THE TWELVE WONDERS

Paolo Debernardi

authorHOUSE®

AuthorHouse™ UK Ltd.
500 Avebury Boulevard
Central Milton Keynes, MK9 2BE
www.authorhouse.co.uk
Phone: 08001974150

First published by AuthorHouse 12/30/2009

ISBN: 978-1-4490-5787-9 (sc)

This book is printed on acid-free paper.

INTRODUCTION

"The twelve wonders" is an English stories book with twelve amazing stories which I am sure the booklover will enjoy reading again and again.

I have never written a story in my own mother tongue. It was very difficult at first as the Italian language was still a big influence in my writing, but with lot of work and dedication I have managed to overcome this difficulty.

In "The twelve wonders" the booklover will enjoy discover different themes: crimes, tragedy, happy ending, sci-fi, fantasy, ghost and etc.

This remarkable book is nice to be shared with other people. Enjoy reading it again and again.

The Author Paolo Debernardi

Acknowledgements

I would like to thank very much AuthorHouse, which without their help my book will never published professionally.

I would like to recommend anyone who has desire to see their work in books or saved digitally, they will look after you like no other Publishers have done.

I would also like to thank very much Amazon, Borders and Waterstone for the national distribution, without them you will not be able to read this amazing book.

CONTENTS

"THEY ALWAYS COME BACK, THEY ALWAYS COME BACK!"

"It was real", Maggie thundered in the silent kitchen.

Brian puzzled, "What do you mean?"

"I saw your dad one year ago", her voice shivered in harmony with her body.

"You know that it's impossible!" Brian shouted.

"I know… I know very well. He died five years ago, but it was him." Maggie replied.

"Nonsense!" Brian exclaimed.

"He came to see me. His gesturing hands, smile, voice. I know it was your dad", Maggie replied.

"I miss him"; her voice broke as her tears fell, "…very much."

"I know mum. I'm sorry"; Brian apologised giving her a handkerchief.

"Don't worry Brian. It's not your fault. Maybe it's better I tell you what happened." Maggie reassured him.

She was shivering more and more, but the more she spoke about it the more there was a sense of relief.

I was reading a book about ten o'clock when… somebody knocked on the door.

I thought, "Who could it be at this time?" I opened the door and the first thing I saw was a thick fog. It was very strange, a thick fog on a summer night. Then a figure appeared out of the fog.

It was an old man. I couldn't describe him very well, because he had a hooded jacket. He was carrying an umbrella.

"Good evening, madam. I am sorry to disturb you. I am a friend of your husband", the stranger smiled.

"Good evening, Sir. Can I help you?" I replied.

"My name is Mr Peter Anderson. Your husband knew me very well. We worked together in the same company"; Peter spoke moving his hands.

"Very strange, my husband never spoke about you. He never kept any secrets from me. Maybe he forgot to tell me about you", I replied.

I liked Peter, even though I had never met him before.

"Can I come in?" Peter asked.

"Yes, of course, come in", I gestured.

"Thank you." We started to speak about my husband, the time of our happiness, you and the past.

I was very surprised at his interest in my husband and at his gesturing hands.

Despite the lights in the house I couldn't see his face.

The clock struck midnight.

I couldn't believe the time had gone by so quickly.

Peter apologised "I am sorry, but it's too late. I have to go. It was a pleasure to meet you. Bye-bye"

"Thank you very much for coming. You remind me of all the best memories of my husband. Bye Peter", my voice was joyful.

I closed the door. His dry umbrella was near my door.

Quickly, I opened the door. "Sorry, Peter, you forgot your umbrella!" I shouted.

I was shocked. The fog had vanished and millions of stars were shining in the sky.

"Never mind, tomorrow I'll phone the company and I'll make an arrangement to give him back his umbrella", I thought.

Closing the door, I switched off the lights going to bed.

The following morning, I phoned the company.

I was shocked to find out that no Peter Anderson had ever worked over there and his umbrella had vanished like the fog the night before.

I started to believe it was he. It was my husband.

"You see Brian, it was your dad. They always come back, they always come back!"

These final words echoed in their minds and it seems they become stronger and stronger on foggy days whispering in the house: "They always come back, they always come back!"

WAITING

Gazing out of the window, Martin was expecting the taxi to arrive, his waiting seemed to last an eternity. The room was completely silent, broken by the thrumming of his heart echoing with the ticking clock.

Unexpected anxieties and doubts concerning Joanne emerged lazily in his mind.

"Perhaps Joanne isn't coming", he murmured.

He was not surprised. She had let him down before on numerous occasions but somehow… somehow he had thought tonight would be different.

As time passed, his doubts increased and his patience weakened. Martin began losing hope. He paced the room, stopping occasionally to absently tap his foot on the bare floorboards, his worried face framed in the dirty glass of upstairs window.

On checking his watch he saw the appointed time was definitely up. Half past seven they had agreed to meet and now it was almost eight.

"She's not coming", he mumbled, "unless she's caught in traffic?" He added as an afterthought, the possibility momentarily raising his spirits. But outside he could see the traffic was light. Rush hour had come and gone. He had to face it; she had let him down again. Would he ever learn?

Staring at his feet depressed, he felt he was dying, then a taxi pulled to a halt across the street. "Hallelujah!" Martin piped. He jumped like a fawn full of life. His heart was full of joy.

Without hesitation he raced out onto the landing and ran downstairs, taking the steps three a time heedless of the danger of his breakneck pace.

"Joanne! Joanne, I knew you'd come this time I knew you wouldn't let me down." But as he drew closer he could see it wasn't his Joanne at all.

"Sorry, love. I'm not Joanne"; the woman said paying off the taxi driver.

"She isn't" "She is forty years old. My Joanne is twenty", he thought.

"Sorry", he said, between gasping breaths. "I have you confused."

"Don't worry, love. She'll be soon here. If I were twenty years younger, I would love to be your darling. You seem a nice guy"

"Thanks" "I think she will never come tonight", he thought.

"Sorry, love, but I have to go, my family is waiting for me." "Bye-bye, love"

"Bye." She was walking away on the opposite direction carrying overfilled shopping bags. She climbed the stairs and entered her house. She was gone like everybody else in his life.

"She is very lucky. She is surrounded by people who will always be there for her!"

"I'm alone", Martin thought.

Martin glanced down the street and saw the taxi was gone. No cars were driving in the street, no one to meet or speak to. Filled with dismay and disappointment he returned to his room. On the way upstairs, one dogged step at a time as if the entire world was on his shoulders,

he reflected that he was truly alone and with a broken heart.

Joanne, the only person he had ever loved, was not coming. He realised she would never come to this house, ever again. He did not blame her though, be blamed himself. He was the one who had been unfaithful and Joanne had discovered the truth, but he hadn't been able to help himself. The one-night-stand had just happened and he had wanted to explain this to Joanne. He wanted to tell her how stupid he had been and how sorry, but it was too late.

At the memory of the first day when they bumped into each other Martin sighed deeply. He was wandering carelessly through a narrow street when his eyes met hers.

It was love at first sight. He was almost certain it would last and now he lost her forever.

The thought of growing old and alone it was unbearable. He could not cope with it. After jotting few verses on a piece of paper. He opened a drawer where his gun had been placed. The touch of the cold revolver sent shivers down his spine, but he was determined. He held it tight and pulled the trigger.

Beside his body, there was a poem titled Joanne.

O Joanne, I miss you so much
Your long blonde hair is sunshine
Breaking through a cloudy sky
You always made me smile.
I miss your blue eyes
Mirror of your love and soul for me
But I lost them for one foolish night.
Goodbye to my only beloved.

A SHOUT FOR INSPECTOR WILSON

"Oh!" a voice shouted. Immediately, leaving the crossword nearly finished, the butler came out from the kitchen to see what had happened.

Dashing up the stairs, he arrived out of breath on the first floor. He heard footsteps becoming lighter in the distance.

He turned his head to the left and saw the tall figure of a woman running away and disappearing in the dark.

The butler rubbed his eyes; he didn't believe what he had seen.

"I think I'm too tired. I need to get some rest"; he thought shrugging his shoulders.

Walking straight to the light coming from a bedroom, he recognised the room.

It was Mr John Smith's bedroom.

Inside the room, Mr Smith's body was lying face down in a pool of blood on the floor.

"Wearing his favourite pyjamas and brown slippers, he was going to bed, but he didn't make it. Poor Mr Smith! Somebody must have shot him. God, bless his soul", the butler thought.

"Oh, Mr Anthony. Mr Smith asked me to take his newspaper in the living room downstairs, but when I came back, I found him lying on the floor, dead! Poor, man", the maid, replied crying. "Mr Anthony, I hope you believe me."

"You know how much I respect Mr Smith. I would never kill him for any reason. He gave me a job. Without his money, my poor family would be dead by now!" she grasped the gun, not to threaten Mr Anthony, but to convince him of her innocence.

"I believe you. I know Mrs Felicity; I know you couldn't have done it. You love everybody." He reassured her.

With a great respect, avoiding any contradiction he said, "Please, put the gun down"

"Yes, Mr Anthony"

"Oh", he sighed with a sense of relief.

Her hands were shaking putting the silencer on the floor.

"She couldn't have killed Mr Smith, her hands were too shaky. She also hates weapons."

Standing up, running towards him, she hugged him crying.

"Don't worry, Mrs Felicity, everything will be fine", Mr Anthony reassured her.

He looked around. Everything was tidy. Except for Mr Smith's body and a pool of blood on the floor, nothing seemed missing.

They regained their composure.

"What can we do now?" Mrs Felicity asked.

"I am going to phone the police, but don't touch anything", Mr Anthony replied.

"Oh, no! I touched the gun. I'm in a big trouble now, Mr Anthony, aren't I?"

"You aren't. You didn't commit any crime. Don't worry, Mrs Felicity. Maybe I know who it is"

"Who? Mr Anthony" A lot of questions came into her small head, but very curious.

"I can't say. I'm not sure"

Mr Anthony disappeared for five minutes.

She was frightened at staying in the same room where Mr Smith was lying dead.

In her head, voices were whispering "murder, murder."

Five minutes were an eternity for her.

Finally, he came back. "The police are on their way, soon they will be here."

She hugged him.

"Don't worry, everything will be fine."

She was very agitated. She was shaking with fear.

"Before I heard voices in my head whispering murder, murder"

"It's only your imagination playing bad tricks"

Silence reigned in the room.

Only the thunder broke it rolling in the distance becoming louder approaching the house.

Black clouds were covering the clear night, hiding it behind their masses.

Thunder crashed above the house with forked lightning.

Mrs Felicity was trembling like a child.

Mr Anthony was not frightened.

The thunder reminded him of all the bombs falling all over the places in the Second War World. The rain was teeming down beating the tiled roof like bullets.

The house lights were flickering on and off.

"Don't be afraid. It's only a bad storm"

"I'm going to check the electric generator. I'll be back very soon", he reassured her.

"All r-r-right, Mr Anthony, but don't be s-s-so l-l-long", Mrs Felicity stammered.

Lightning struck near the house brightening a branch making her jump.

When it seemed nothing was going to happen, the doorbell rang.

It was half an hour later. "The police are here", Mr Anthony thought. Coming out of the kitchen, he hurried to unlock the door.

There were two men on the doorstep.

One was in his forties with a bristling moustache, wearing a waterproof coat and smoking his pipe.

By his side a youth in his late teens, with red short hair, also wearing a coat, but completely soaked.

"Good evening, I'm Inspector Wilson. This is my assistant Constable George Brown. I guess you're the person who called me."

"Good evening, Inspector Wilson, Constable George Brown. I'm Mr Anthony, the butler. Please, come in"

"Thank you", they replied.

Mr Anthony closed the door behind them.

"Can I take your coats, please?" Mr Anthony asked.

They took off their coats. Mr Anthony hung them on the hallstand.

"Thank you, Inspector Wilson, for coming tonight. I called you, because my master, Mr John Smith has been killed"

"I'm not sure who killed him, but if you and your assistant follow me upstairs, I will explain everything to you"

"All right, Mr Anthony, show me the way", Inspector Wilson replied.

They walked up the stairs, turned right and went inside John Smith's bedroom.

Inspector Wilson was very surprised.

He expected the murder room to be in chaos pretending there had been a burglary, instead of premeditated homicide.

But the room was tidy. "Very strange", Inspector Wilson thought touching his bristling moustache, "I don't understand why the killer didn't set up a burglary. On the other hand, he could be a beginner"

"Mrs Felicity, I would like to introduce you, Inspector Wilson and Constable George Brown. She is Mr John Smith's maid", Mr Anthony explained.

"Good evening, Sirs"

"Good evening, madam"

Inspector Wilson looked at her.

Mrs Felicity felt all the attention was on her.

"Whatever I say or do, they will never believe me. Even more maybe they already think I'm guilty", Mrs Felicity thought staring at her feet.

"She couldn't have killed her master. She is too shocked. She looks like a frightened animal. If she did, why she didn't run away? Why she didn't throw away the gun? Choosing instead to leave the gun on the floor? The finger would seem to be pointed at her! No, she's innocent. She's guilty of being in a wrong place", Inspector Wilson thought.

"Sorry Sir", Constable George Brown interrupted Inspector Wilson's thoughts.

"Mr John Smith was murdered when he turned his back on the killer"

"There is a deep wound in his back. I believe he was laughing before he was killed, because the corners of his mouth are still turned up", Constable George Brown explained.

"Mr John Smith knew the killer. It could be a man or a woman. So when he or she came into his room, something very peculiar happened to make him laugh. The killer misinterpreted his laugh, thinking he was mocking him. He took out the gun, fired a shot and ran away. Doesn't make any sense!" Inspector Wilson thought.

"Constable George Brown, take all the finger prints in the room and on the gun", Inspector Wilson said.

"All right, Sir" "I killed him", Mrs Felicity shouted.

"Don't be stupid, Mrs Felicity, you didn't", Mr Anthony said very angry. "Inspector Wilson, don't believe Mrs Felicity. She is too shocked at the moment. She grasped the gun before, not to threaten me, but to convince me of her innocence. It was a moment of weakness", Mr Anthony explained.

"Don't worry, Mrs Felicity, I don't believe for one moment, you killed your master", Inspector Wilson reassured her.

"Don't you?" she asked.

"Yes, I don't have any doubts. You are not capable", Inspector Wilson explained.

"Oh", she sighed with a sense of relief.

"Mr Anthony, can you reconstruct the evening before Mr John Smith was killed?" Inspector Wilson asked.

"Yes, of course, Inspector Wilson. It was half past ten. I was doing a crossword in the kitchen when I heard a shout coming from upstairs. I dashed up the stairs on reaching the first floor. I heard footsteps becoming lighter in the distance I turned my head to the left and saw the figure of a tall woman, running away and disappearing in the dark. I thought it was Mrs Felicity, but she was taller and more athletic.

I rubbed my eyes; I couldn't believe what I saw.

I thought I was too tired and needed to get some rest.

Afterwards I went into Mr John Smith's bedroom. He was lying face down in a pool of blood, wearing his favourite pyjamas and brown slippers. I didn't touch anything, except for the silencer when Mrs Felicity grasped it. She spoke to me crying.

I looked around, but the room was tidy and nothing seemed missing. Then I called you and now here we are", Mr Anthony explained.

"Thank you, Mr Anthony. Mrs Felicity, do you have anything to add to the reconstruction?" Inspector Wilson asked.

"Yes, Inspector Wilson, Mr Smith was calm and happy when he asked me to bring his newspaper from the living room downstairs. I wish I had been faster returning with it! He could be still alive", she said very sadly.

"Don't be silly, it's not your fault. Maybe then we would have two corpses, instead of one", Inspector Wilson reassured her.

"Please, Mrs Felicity, carry on", Inspector Wilson asked.

"I came back after ten minutes and I found him lying on the floor, dead", she replied.

"Did you hear anything or see anybody?" Inspector Wilson asked.

"No, Inspector"

"Thank you. It's very weird, very difficult case. Mr Anthony, you told me nothing seems to be missing, are you sure?"

"Not really"

"Mr Anthony, did you check the safe?" Mrs Felicity asked.

"No, did you?"

"No, I don't know the combination", Mrs Felicity replied.

Mr Anthony moved a painting. Opening the safe, he was dumbfounded.

"It's missing. Mr John Smith's will is missing, but who could have stolen it?" Mr Anthony said.

"Do you know anybody who would be interested in stealing Mr Smith's will?" Inspector Wilson asked.

"Yes, one person. His son, Mr Peter Smith, but at the moment, he is in London on business. He will be back next week. But he could not possibly be the killer"

"Nothing is impossible in life", Inspector Wilson thought.

"Suppose he is guilty, why does he want his father dead?" Inspector Wilson asked.

"Because, his father hated him. On his death, Mr Peter Smith doesn't inherit anything. All the properties will be sold and all the proceeds will be donated to charity", Mr Anthony explained.

"Ah, I see", Inspector Wilson, replied.

There was a new light in his eyes.

Something was becoming clearer in his mind.

Before it was very cloudy, but now sunshine was breaking through.

"Let me see, if I've got it right. If Mr John Smith dies and his will disappears, his son will inherit everything"

"I suppose so, Inspector Wilson"

"Mr Anthony, did you know about this gun?"

"I know Mr Peter Smith had a similar gun, but he lost it two years ago"

"I understand" "At the moment I can't prove anything. I need more evidence."

"Mr Anthony, you told me you saw the figure of a tall woman disappearing in the dark. Can you show me the corridor?" Inspector Wilson asked touching his bristling moustache.

"Yes, Inspector Wilson. Please, gentlemen, follow me. I will show you the way"

They walked out of the room.

In the right corridor there was no doors on either side, no window at the bottom of the corridor.

"How could the killer get out?" Inspector Wilson thought.

"Constable George Brown, check for hollow walls. There must be a secret panel somewhere"

Constable George Brown started knocking on the walls. After a while, nearly at the end of the corridor, the wall gave an empty sound. On this wall, Inspector Wilson noticed a painting that had been moved from its original position leaving a black mark. He put it back. Suddenly, there appeared an opening between the walls.

Mr Anthony was very surprised.

It was completely dark. "Constable George Brown, switch on your torch", Inspector Wilson said.

"Mr Anthony, you stay here, it could be dangerous"

"All right, Inspector Wilson"

They held their guns as they entered the opening.

It was a corridor. Constable George Brown lit everywhere. Something was shining on the floor. Inspector Wilson picked it up. It was a gold lighter with two initials P and S at the bottom.

"Mr Anthony, it's all clear. Now you can come in"

Mr Anthony entered. "Mr Anthony, did you know about this corridor?"

"No, Inspector Wilson"

"I see. I wonder where it leads. We're going to find out... We'll be back very soon"

Ten minutes later, they came back.

"Mr Anthony, I found other evidence, but at the moment, I will not arrest anybody, because I want to speak to Mr Peter Smith, first"

"All right, Inspector Wilson"

"Mr Anthony, I would like to ask you a favour"

"Yes, certainly, Inspector Wilson"

"Could you tell Peter Smith, I suspect Mrs Felicity of killing his father. Yes, we know she didn't, but I want him to believe he got off scot-free"

"Certainly, Inspector Wilson", Mr Anthony smiled.

"Thank you, we'll be back in a week's time"

Inspector Wilson moved the painting and the opening closed.

The police officers then left the house.

After the shock, Mr Anthony and Mrs Felicity went to bed in their respective rooms.

In the house, it was very busy. Mr Peter Smith was supposed to be coming back after a week, but he turned up few days later.

He started giving orders to his servants like a general to his soldiers. Mr Anthony and Mrs Felicity felt they were puppets in his hands. How they missed their master.

"You're going to have to get a move on, if you wish to remain in my service", urged Peter Smith.

"Sorry, Mr Smith"

"Don't waste time talking, clean my shoes"

The doorbell rang. "Leave it, open the door! Hurry up! It could be my boss", Mr Peter Smith shouted.

It wasn't his boss. Inspector Wilson and Constable George Brown were at the door. When Mr Anthony opened it, he had a sense of relief seeing them. He smiled.

"Who is it?" Mr Peter Smith asked very angry.

"The police are here. Inspector Wilson and Constable George Brown", Mr Anthony replied.

"Don't stand at the door! Let them in! What an earth are you doing? You are dismissed"

Mr Anthony walked away depressed.

"I'm sorry, Inspector Wilson and Constable George Brown, it's very difficult to find reliable and efficient servants, nowadays they are so clumsy. Please, forgive him for his rudeness."

"Can I help you? Inspector Wilson"

"Maybe as you know, we suspect Mrs Felicity of killing your father"

"Yes, terrible woman"

"But, I suspect another person too"

"Who?"

"Can we speak in private?" Inspector Wilson asked.

"Yes, certainly. We can go to the living room, over there"

They went to the living room and sat on the sofa.

"Would you like a drink?" Mr Peter Smith asked.

"No, I'm sorry, we can't, we are in duty. Thank you"

"You don't mind if I have one"

"Oh, no"

Peter Smith prepared a gin and tonic with some ice.

"As a routine, we have to ask you some questions. Do you mind?"

"No, of course, I'm very happy to help your inquiries"

"Where were you when your father died?"

"I was in London on business all week. I mean I had intended to stay all week, but when I phoned home two days ago, I was told the tragic news so I decided to go home"

"I see"

"Could you give me the telephone number of the hotel?" Inspector Wilson asked.

"I can give you a card from the hotel, there is also the telephone number. But why do you ask? You don't believe I travelled four hundred miles to kill my father. That would be ridiculous. Everybody knows we didn't have a good relationship, but to think I kill my father. It is preposterous"

16

"We will see", Inspector Wilson thought.

"Phone my colleague in London. Ask him to check Mr Peter Smith's alibi", Inspector Wilson whispered to Constable George Brown.

"I'm sorry, gentlemen, I have a duty to attend to. I'll be back shortly."

Constable George Brown left.

Peter Smith thought "Something is going on, but I don't know what"

"Can I ask you a few more questions?"

"Yes, but I don't see any reason. I told you I was in London on business. I can prove it!"

"Do you have a car?"

"Like everybody else"

"What make of car is it?"

"It's a luxury car"

"Silver, Mercedes-Benz 300sl, number plate R756LYN"

"Yes, how do you know?"

"A farmer saw your car, on the road after half past ten two nights ago"

"It's impossible. I was in London at that time. Maybe the farmer was sniffing drugs or invented something, because he is jealous of me. Nobody loves me in this village"

"You are walking on thin ice! You were here that night. Your car can prove it. This witness saw your car. He wasn't sniffing drugs or make up a false story. He's a very reliable person. You are not", Inspector Wilson thought.

"Do you have a silencer?"

"Yes, I had one, but I lost it. I never declared I had lost it"

"You're a liar. You never lost it. You were only hiding it in your house", Inspector Wilson thought.

"Did it look like this?"

"Yes, it looks like mine, but obviously, it's not"

"Do you have a lighter? My matches are running out"

Mr Peter Smith checked in his pocket, but he didn't find it.

"Are you looking for this?"

"I don't know what are you talking about?"

"Very strange, I thought you were looking for yours"

"Yes, but now I remember I threw it away last year. I was a smoker, but then I gave up smoking so I didn't want to keep it, in case I should be tempted to start again. Maybe its Mr Anthony's lighter"

"It's pity he doesn't smoke. How can you explain the marks P and S? It's obvious. It's yours. You try too hard, but you don't convince me. Sooner or later you will make a mistake", Inspector Wilson thought.

"So what do you think about this homicide, Mr Smith?"

"I think the killer was very stupid to forget to set up a burglary and shoot my father in his back"

"How could you possibly know these details? I didn't tell you", Inspector Wilson thought.

"Mr Peter Smith, you have a lot to explain", Constable George Brown said re-entering the living room.

"Inspector Wilson, I don't know what your assistant is talking about? Can you ask him to calm down?"

"No, let him speak"

"Thank you, Sir"

"Apparently, nobody knows anything about your business in London. The manager of the hotel told me it was your holiday. Also nobody saw you there two nights ago. All the staff on duty over there saw a person who was wearing the same clothes as yours, but they didn't see the face. You booked a room for two nights before Mr Smith died. Afterwards, you never came back. I also questioned Mr Anthony about your phone call. It was not from London, but from a hotel in a nearby village. He heard the name of the hotel in the background of the phone call. I checked it and found out you had booked a room for two nights after your father had been killed"

"I don't what are you talking about! I was in London on business. That is the truth"

"I think I know what happened that night"

"I would like to know as well as you"

"You came here that night, but you couldn't go inside the house wearing your clothes, because you wouldn't have an alibi. In London your friend wore clothes like yours, meanwhile you changed yours and wore woman clothes. Afterwards, you used the corridor which connected the outside to the inside the house.

You waited for the right moment, while Mrs Felicity was away. You came out from the opening, went straight to your father's bedroom. Your plan was to kill him and steal his will, because if you did that, you inherited all the estate.

On the other hand if your father died, all the estate would be sold and the proceeds would be donated to charity.

When he saw you, he laughed. You couldn't stand his cruel behaviour any more. Also you didn't want to risk anybody seeing you kill your father. So when he turned his back, shot him, stole his will, hid yourself until Mrs Felicity came into the room and ran away."

"You have a lot of imagination, you can't prove anything"

"Your alibi is over. All the evidence is pointed at you. The silencer was in your father's bedroom, your father's will disappeared, the lighter lost in the corridor. The farmer saw you car. Your tyre marks from your car left on the road. We took some samples. We have only to match with your tyres and they will prove I am right. And finally you mentioned the killer shot your father in his back. I didn't tell you this detail."

"All right, I will speak", Peter Smith, said, sweating for the first time in his life.

He was no longer in control.

"Before you say something. You are entitled to a solicitor and whatever you say it could be used against you in court"

"I killed him. You are quite right, except you don't know why I shot him. I wanted to take my revenge. He used violence on me when I was young. Then I couldn't stand him any more. He always treated me like a loser. He was rich. I am poor. I had to kill him in order to have my rightful inheritance. When I entered his room, he started to laugh and tell me he would never give me any more money. I depended on his money. So I took out my gun from my pocket when he turned his back. I shot him. I don't regret it. He deserved it" Peter Smith said showing his wrists.

"You are under arrest, Mr Peter Smith"; Constable George Brown replied putting handcuffs on his wrists.

Constable George Brown took him in the police car; meanwhile Inspector Wilson wanted to speak to Mr Anthony.

"Now what will happen to you and Mrs Felicity?" Inspector Wilson asked.

"I don't know. We will find another job. We can't stay here, all the estate will be sold", Mr Anthony replied.

"Take care both of you. All the best"

"Thank you, Inspector Wilson. Goodbye, now"

The police car sped away.

Mr Anthony became a gardener and Mrs Felicity worked as a waitress in a restaurant. Most of the estate was sold, except for the house.

Nobody was interested in buying it.

There was hearsay that something very weird was going in the house.

Lights were switched on and off, voices were echoing in the house and objects were moving without any possible explanation. But nobody was living over there.

Somebody suggested that the house could be haunted.

Some say that John Smith's ghost is laughing, because his son killed him and stole his will. Yet, in the end it was the son who lost everything.

DELTA CENTAURI

It was 19 June 1994. I remembered it very well like it was yesterday. As my everyday habit, I was jogging after a delicious, but calorific meal, in the park.

The sky was so breathtaking with the moon and stars shining that I stopped running to admire it. The park was silent. It was very peculiar. It was a summer night so I expected birds singing and cicadas shrilling, but that night was completely different from the others. Something was going to happen.

I felt it on my skin. The waiting and spooky atmosphere increased my fears enormously. On my skin goose bumps appeared. Although I felt uncomfortable I didn't want to run away. I felt there was a presence to reassuring me to stay calm. I took a long breath and my confidence increased.

At this particular moment, a bluish mist was coming in my direction. I had never seen anything like that. I was sure it didn't belong to our world.

It could be coming from outer space.

Slowly and curiously I started to walk up to the unusual mist. I was frightened, but a voice was whispering telepathically in my head: "Don't be afraid, I won't hurt you"

The mist was very thin and dispersive.

After walking for five minutes, I was delighted and shocked. A metallic triangular flying saucer landed in the park. I always wished to see a flying saucer closer, but I had never been so lucky until now.

I knew a lot of unidentified flying objects had been sighted all over the world in the last few years and I believed they existed. But one thing is to have faith, another is seeing in reality.

I rubbed my eyes. I wanted to be sure it wasn't a hallucination or dream. But it wasn't. It was real.

I was so excited, but at the same time terrified. I didn't know what to do.

The aliens could friends helping us to save our planet or enemies looking for a New World to conquer.

With these doubts in my mind, in the front of the spacecraft a door opened.

I swallowed my saliva nervously. From the flying saucer, a tall figure came out. Some drops of sweat rolled down from my forehead.

It was a medium built alien wearing a silver suit and gold helmet.

"Don't worry, I'm not dangerous. Please come closer", he spoke telepathically.

"I'm scared, but I don't know why I feel you are sincere and friendly"

"I know. You don't have anything to fear. I come in peace. I want to become your friend"

"Me too"

Approaching him, I felt very calm and all my anxiety was gone.

I felt reassured to see his positive body language. His three-finger hand showed the way inside his spacecraft and underneath his gold helmet I could glimpse a sweet and friendly smile.

Inside the flying saucer everything looked different from what I had expected outside. His external outline gave an impression to well-defined shape, but I was completely wrong. The inside was all opposite. The white walls and the long corridors linking to the huge rooms gave a sensation of infinity.

In each room, there was a lot of activity. Computer operators coming from different planets were working together in harmony in a friendly atmosphere; meanwhile men, women and children were following other aliens like mine.

I asked him a lot of questions about these operators, but he was vague. He only told me they came from all the planets of the Universe.

"You see your species is very violent and dangerous. We have to select all human beings we want to contact. You are afraid of us and in your mind you think we want to conquer your planet. We used to be like you three hundred years ago, but then we developed with superior visitors' help, which modified our society. Nowadays in my planet, we live together in harmony and peace.

With our help, your species will reach the same stage in the future and maybe you or the next generation won't be surprised to see visitors coming from all over the Universe working and living together", he said.

"How great it will be! New contacts, new friends I can't wait"

"Be patient, the time hasn't come yet"

He was pleased to hear that I was thrilled at our shared future.

Then my curiosity spoilt everything. Sometimes I wish I could shut my mouth.

I asked him where all the human beings go and at this question he became very upset.

"You don't have to worry about them. Nothing will happen. We need them for a wonderful project. You see we come for a planet completely different from yours. In our planet, all the vegetation and water was destroyed by chemical elements. Fortunately, we survived, because we adapted our bodies to the changes. So we have to wear our suit and helmet to protect us from solar radiation and germs, which can kill us. Without these protections we can't live on your planet"

"So why can't they change their bodies to adapt to our environment?" "They have technology and knowledge. They have already achieved this in their planet."

"We can't. We tried, but we failed. Your body is so complex and evolved we can't succeed. We need your help"

"I'll help you"

We entered a room where there was a black table in the centre. It looked very solid like a stone and it gave me an impression of being cold.

He approached another alien and together they had a brief conversation telepathically.

Then he came back and reassured me.

"Don't be afraid! You will have some tests, but you won't feel any pain or fear"

I undressed as he asked me and I lay on the table completely naked.

The table was very soft and warm giving the sensation of being on a bed.

From the wall a flat machine appeared, scanned my body and disappeared. It was a very strange sensation, but afterwards I felt all my pain and fear were gone. I was relaxed.

A long tube came out from the side of the table. It stimulated my male organ and sucked my sperms away.

"We need your sperm to combine human chromosomes with ours. Only in this way will our babies be able to live in your planet in the future"

I felt miserable to be treated as guinea pig. I prefer to make love naturally, instead of artificially. But I couldn't really complain about it. I'd be a father.

The tube disappeared and a long thin silver tube appeared. It went inside my nose. The operation lasted briefly and was painless. It came out from my nose and vanished.

It was all over. He reassured me and allowed me to dress.

"It was for your own good. You had a terrible illness, but my machine removed it. Now I would like to show you where I come from. Please follow me"

"Yes, sure"

I followed him. We entered another room, which was covered by maps about the constellations and galaxies of the Universe.

He pointed to a planet.

"I come from Delta Centauri in a planet called "Ursula". It is 5 light-years from Earth. I come in peace. I want to protect your planet from nuclear self-destruction or a meteorite impact"

He carried on explaining, but my mind was completely full of information. I remembered only I peered out at another room. There were human children playing with young aliens.

They were enjoying so much they were laughing and running.

Then everything was blank. I don't remember anything. Maybe they remove my experience from my head.

I found myself on the grass in the park. In that particular instant, the only thing I remembered was the bluish mist, but not the flying saucer and the following events. I looked at my watch.

It was 11 o'clock. There were three hours missing. I didn't remember how and where I spent them.

Not finding any explanation, I decided to go home.

The following morning, I panicked to see drops of blood coming out from my nose. It was very weird. I was so alarmed that I went straight to the hospital where I had a check-up.

The doctor was surprised to find out there was a chance of cancer in my head, but now it had gone mysteriously. There was only a strange unidentified piece of metal in my head. I explained to the doctor that I had never been operated. I didn't know where it was coming from.

He suggested going to the psychiatrist, because it could be a case of alien abduction.

At first I was reluctant to go. Who could believe me? They could think I was mad. Then I changed my mind. I was too curious. I wanted to give it a go. I made an appointment.

After several retro hypnoses, I relived my experience. I couldn't remember it, because it was hidden in my memory. But afterwards it was recalled. I remembered the end of my experience. I was on the grass looking at the spacecraft flying away at high speed in the sky.

The psychiatrist introduced me to his friend, who was abducted by aliens, to share my experience with other people.

This is the reason I am here tonight. At last, I would like to say it is a real story. I didn't invent anything. It really happened to me. I know there are many people, who deceived others with incredible stories coming from their fervid imagination. But I'm not like them. This is real life.

Every night I wake up, screaming from this nightmare.

Later that night, the expert thought before writing in a file "I believe it is a genuine story. The witness is honest, sincere and objective". Then he put it in a drawer together with hundreds of the other files. They all told the same story.

THE INCREDIBLE TONY

"Help, help" a little girl was screaming in the strong and cold river Ice.

No one seemed to hear her. They were staring at her petrified on the riverbank.

Only Tony standing on the bridge 5 feet above was ready for action.

In a split second he jumped from the bridge and dived into the river heedless of danger.

For a couple of minutes there was no trace of Tony.

Some women were starting to cry and others were looking down very depressed as the last hope of rescuing the little girl vanished.

In this moment of despair he appeared on the surface.

The tears of sadness turned into tears of joy.

Some people jumped and cheered him on and some others applauded him.

With powerful strokes his arms and legs were cutting through the current of the river like a salmon.

"Don't be afraid, everything will be all right" with calm words Tony reassured the little girl approaching her. She sighed with a sense of relief and smiled for the first time.

He put an arm around her. She stopped shivering and looked at him who smiled back. He was swimming slower and the journey seemed to be endless. She was very glad to feel the sand of the riverbank where a paramedic was standing by holding a blanket in his arm. The paramedic came close to her, wrapping her with the blanket and drying her hair. The crowd was still applauding and cheering Tony on. He was very calm and his clothes appeared not to be wet at all.

A forty-year-old woman approached the little girl with anxiety and rage.

"What were you thinking of to pick the ball up in the deep water? Did you know the current of the river Ice is so strong and cold?" the worried woman asked.

"I know mum" the little girl replied between tears.

" I would take it easy on her. She was so frightened," Tony said looking her mother. His eyes had a brief blue sparkling light.

The anxious woman winked in a way to say thank you. Now she was very calm and all her worries and aggression were completely gone.

She and her daughter walked homc holdings hands. The little girl turned her head for the last time and winked at Tony.

"Well done Tony! You have rescued that little girl from drowning. You have saved the day again!" the crowd was shouting. "You are our hero!" other people were saying.

"He is just a mad man"

"I agree. Why would he risk his life to save that little girl?"

"He doesn't even know her and her mother is very poor. How could she pay him back?"

Two older men were whispering behind the crowd.

Tony saw them and replied to the crowd.

"I am not a hero. I am an ordinary man who loves helping people. That is what I am."

"Don't be silly Tony. Did you forget what you did yesterday?" Constable Ross Chapman asked.

"No, I cannot forget" Tony replied.

Tony is thinking I am an ordinary man.

In reality he is extraordinary.

4 feet 10 tall with wide shoulders, marine biceps, short muscular and firm legs Tony is very strong as well as agile and fast. Even more unusual he has a sparkling light in his blue eyes when he helps people in danger. They feel relaxed and calm after they see it.

In his heart he knows he is a friend to everyone and helping people making him feel so good.

They feel good too and thank him with every kind of present. He always accepts them with a smile.

This is not the first time the inhabitants of his village Ice had seen his act of heroism. Every single day something terrible happens in the village and Tony always saves the day. He is always on the lips of people for his bravery and kindness.

Nobody can forget what Tony had done the day before.

There was a fire in his friend's house and a baby was in the bedroom. Lucy could not help the baby because the fire was blocking the door. So she ran out and called for help. The fire brigades were extinguishing another fire in a neighbouring city and therefore they would not arrive in time.   Lucy was horrified and shocked. She was crying begging people to save her baby. None came out to rescue her baby except Tony. Without any hesitation he entered the house on fire and ran up the stairs.

A couple of minutes later he walked out with her baby in his arms.

Both Tony and the baby were safe and sound. Lucy was very grateful and she was smiling, even though her beautiful house was burnt down.

An unusually cold wind was blowing in this hottest day of summer.

Tony waved goodbye to everyone on the riverbank. He felt shivers down his spine. He knew that was a bad sign. It meant something terrible would happen to him and he could not do anything about it. He carried on walking to the entrance of the bank before stepped inside he looked onto the main street.

There was a crowd waving and applauding him by way of saying thank you for rescuing the little girl in the river.

He smiled back with a strange sadness.

Inside the bank it was very chaotic.

A lot of people were queuing at the counter with payslips and bills. Lucy was there as well. She was so beautiful with her blonde hair tied back and the new red dress up to her knees. She smiled.

In this sweet moment the door of the bank opened violently, a short man wearing a balaclava thundered into the hall carrying a shining semiautomatic gun and a plastic bag.

With a distinct husky voice he thundered: "Nobody will get hurt if everyone follows my demands!!" pointing the gun at the crowd.

"Lie down on the floor, everyone!!"

All the people were terrified. Some young children and women were crying on the floor. Others were too frightened to react.

Tony was observing. He did not want to put anyone in danger. He understood the gunman was frantic.

The last thing he wanted was someone getting hurt.

"Put all the money in the bag" the gunman shouted to the clerk.

"If I were in you I would run. The police will arrive soon and you will be nicked"

"Shut up! Shut up! If you don't shut up, I'll shoot someone!"

"Lie down on the floor or the young woman beside you will die!"

Lucy was petrified at the thought of being shot.

The gunman's hand was shaking and a drop of sweat fell down his forehead.

He was loosing control of his nerves.

In an insane state of mind he pulled the trigger of the semiautomatic and a bullet was released.

In a split second Tony put himself between the bullet and Lucy. Some people screamed at the shot. The bullet hit his chest.

Lucy stopped Tony from falling behind and lay his body down on the floor.

"Do not be afraid, everything will be fine" Tony reassured Lucy with a warm smile.

In the meantime the sound of the police sirens were clearly audible outside. There were a lot of people coming and going.

In this confusion the gunman saw a chance to escape. He took the money and ran out from the back door but the police were waiting for him.

Several reply shots were heard then silence.

Lucy took her courage in both hands and walked out of the bank looking for help.

An ambulance was outside. Two paramedics came out and approached Lucy who was very agitated and confused.

"There is a man who has been shot. There is a man who has been shot" Lucy was saying repeatedly.

"Show us the way, madam"

Lucy showed them the way into the bank.

She was dumfounded.

Tony was not there anymore. Instead dust and a bullet were on the floor where Tony should have been. Lucy could not understand. She was in shock.

She asked to everyone where Tony was. No one could tell her. Some said they did not know who he was. Others were still horrified by the terrible experience.

This tragedy spread wildfire. Everyone was talking about it.

The inhabitants of the neighbouring villages could not believe a man of such bravery and kindness had ever really lived.

They thought he was a fruit of imagination or a legend by the inhabitants of the village Ice, but everyone of them knew Tony was real and he died doing the thing he loved most helping people.

THRILLER IN THE SCARY NIGHT

Lucy knew she should have not walked in the scary alley. She could not help it. She had finished a very long day at work in the cafeteria and she was not thinking straight.

The narrow alley was filthy with rubbish, dead rats and decomposed food.

The place stank so badly Lucy fell nauseous.

The police had reported on many occasions a lot of women had disappeared in the last few years. Someone suggested the abductor was hiding somewhere ready to strike again making the alley very unsafe.

All these women would eventually reappear naked and dead with cuts and bruises on their bodies. The police found they were sexually assaulted before being fatally stabbed with a long knife.

Lucy felt very uncomfortable walking through the alley. She wanted to go through as quickly as possible. The alley was between old damage factories, which had not been used for years. So even if she was in danger and shouting for help no one would ever come to rescue her.

The alley was very long and there was no way to escape so she had to walk to the other side.

She heard a noise behind her. A light footstep was in the distance. She stopped. The noise stopped as well. She began to walk again and the footsteps were much louder. She started to walk more quickly but the mysterious stranger increased the speed to keep up.

Lucy looked back and said, "Who is there?"

No one replied.

Lucy started to cry and get agitated. She was so frightened. She glanced back and saw a shadow on the wall.

Her walk became a run but the mysterious stranger did not give up the chase and he began to run faster and faster.

Lucy could feel her heart beating in her chest. Her breath became heavier. She knew she could not hide anywhere or turn anywhere to escape from the mysterious stranger. She felt she was like an animal in a cage.

She glanced back for the third time and now the shadow was bigger. She could see the shadow was holding something in its right hand. She could not make out what it was. She assumed it was a knife. The metallic blade vibrated in the air making Lucy tremble violently.

The mysterious stranger was gaining on Lucy. She felt her chances to survival were becoming slimmer and slimmer. The mysterious stranger was almost behind her ready to strike.

Lucy saw the exit of the alley in front of her. Her eyes filled with joy. With her last attempt to survive she pushed her tired legs to the extreme.

Lucy collided against a body in front of her. She was lying on the floor. Thinking the mysterious stranger had managed to be in front of her, she began to crawl backwards from him.

" Are you ok, madam?" the policeman said with a warm smile.

"I'm fine, thanks" Lucy replied with a relieved smile after catching her breath.

"Please take my hand, I will help you to stand up"

She was so happy to see a policeman in this area. She felt so safe now. She gave her hand and the policeman helped her.

"Have you walked down the alley?"

"Yes, I did"

"Did you know it is dangerous?"

"Yes, I heard. It was my mistake. I realised I was in the alley half way. Have you seen anyone coming out from the alley except me?"

"No madam, why did you?"

"I thought someone was chasing me with a knife"

"I can assure you no one came out from the alley except you. Tonight, I am patrolling this area to make it safe"

"I feel safe now thanks for being here"

"It is my duties, madam. I hope you have a safe journey"

"Thanks officer"

Lucy felt better even though she escaped from the danger. She felt not completely comfortable. There was a weird feeling the mysterious stranger could have followed her. She was walking in the main square where a lot of people were still out. She tried to look at their shadow to see if she could recognise the one, who had chased her earlier, but they were absolutely different. Even she tried to smell the air or hear the footsteps. None of them matched her memory.

There was not a trace of the mysterious stranger, Lucy was still very careful walking in the main street and taking the bus to go home.

She did not want to be off her guard. She was staring at anyone she could see and the people looked at her in surprise.

She was feeling more confident of herself after she recognised her street. She began to have more strength and she knew no one could harm her now. Her husband was home to protect her. No one would dare to enter her house and violate her.

She sighed with a sense of relief.

She walked out of the bus and walked for a brief moment. The street was very quiet. No one was walking except her. She smiled. She put the key in the front door and turned it. She opened it and closed behind her.

She put her head against the cold doorframe. She was so pleased to be home. She was not longer in danger. She was safe now turning the key.

Lucy was wrong about being safe. Someone was bashing the doorframe violently. She put her hand in front of her mouth in terror. The maniac pulled up the letterbox and let the knife inside. The knife was looking for her. It only found the letterbox and not being satisfied attacked the doorframe.

Lucy shouted "Help, Steve". Her voice echoed in the empty house. She forgot. Steve was on holiday and he would not be back until the following day. She was alone and frightened like a child.

A neighbour's dog was barking awakened by the noise.

Lucy ran on the bare wood stairs but slipped injuring her knee.

The maniac left the front door and smashed the back door. Lucy was trying to crawl forward with difficulties. Her knee was badly injured. She looked at the maniac. "I know you"

That were the last words she said. The maniac stabbed her several times leaving her body lifeless and in a pool of blood. He started to cut her beautiful red dress. He sexually touched her cold body. In his sick state of mind he was enjoying himself.

Then he stopped. He heard the police sirens. There were a lot of people surrounding the house. He stood up rooted to the floor knowing there was no escape.

Two officers entered the house from the back door and jumped on the maniac disarming and handcuffing him.

"Inspector, it is all clear"

"Well done officers! We have captured the maniac who has frightened the city for so long"

"You! I cannot believe it's you! You are the best officer in the force. You have arrested so many criminals and the public love you"

"Why, Constable George Brown, have you killed all these women?" the inspector looked with eyes so intense they seemed to take fire.

"I don't know sir. I have this animal instinct in me. I do not know what I was doing"

"Take him away. Away from me"

The two officers took George Brown to the police car.

"Why would such a great officer do this? Look at this beautiful woman. She doesn't deserve to die" looking at her with eyes full of tears covering her cold body with a blanket.

"THE DEATH TRAP"

Andrew knew since his childhood what he would become as a grown up. He was a determined boy who would have his mind up despite the many difficulties and problems he would face he would carry on his dream and no one or nothing would ever stop him.

No one knew exactly what Andrew would become as he never told to anyone not even to his family, his big brother or closest best friends. He was not shy or shamed at all. He hated people laughing at him for his choices or talking behind his back. His family, big brother and closest best friends were worst of all, as they would interrogate and discourage him if they knew his dream.

That is why he kept it as a secret.

His family eventually would ask him about his future. Of all his family, his dad was keener to ask.

"Andrew, my son, what would you like to become as a grown up?"

It was very difficult for little Andrew not to tell his dad. He wanted to tell the entire world his dream. It was on tip of his tongue and he wanted to scream, but he was so used to keeping the secret he would answer back "I am not sure dad" "I have so many dreams I have not decided yet what I would do"

It did not help at all to keep the secret. His family thought Andrew was an undecided child and he would not accomplish anything in life.

They were wrong.

He was obsessed with his dream he would do anything.

"Dad, I have decided I do not want any presents for Christmas or my birthday"

"Why so?" his dad stared at him puzzled. "Let me check if you have a temperature" putting his hand on Andrew's forehead. Andrew's forehead was cold as ice, but his eyes were so sparkling as if they were saying, "I mean it dad. Just do it"

"Dad, just give me pocket money instead"

"Ok son if you are happy"

"I am dad. Trust me"

Any money Andrew received he saved it all. Not one of the kids and adults would know where Andrew would spend it. He would do it secretly.

At the age of 10, he read an ad in the local paper shop. They were looking for a paperboy. He applied and got the job. He delivered the papers before school and after. The wage was not great despite the weather, it was raining almost every day, and the salary £2.00 an hour Mondays to Saturdays, Andrew was not complaining at all.

He was very excited. "One step closer to fulfilling my dream" He repeated to himself.

One day Peter saw him carrying heavy bags and strange metallic parts.

Peter was Andrew's best friend and classmate. They had known each other since they were 2 years old. They played together in the playground as batman and robin and cowboys.

They confided in each other. They had never been secrets between them as they always told each other everything. Which girl and sport they liked and talked about everything until one day… Peter asked Andrew "what would you do as a grown up?"

Andrew looked at Peter with a sad face. Andrew really liked Peter very much. He considered him as the twin brother he never had. He could not tell him about his dream. He never said one word.

Since then the attitude of Andrew changed drastically. They never talked to each other like before.

They avoided each other though they were in the same classroom. It seemed like they were complete strangers.

"Do you need any help Andrew?"

"No thanks" Andrew replied very crossly. He was afraid that if Peter could see everything in the bag he would tell everyone and the entire village would know. The village was full of noisy and eavesdropping neighbours who enjoyed talking behind people's backs.

Peter did not like Andrew's behaviour. He found it very irritating and annoying. He hoped with time that Andrew would change for the better so they could become friends again. Peter did not understand why Andrew had changed and he thought it was his fault. After a long turning over his mind, he believed it wasn't. "I did not do anything wrong". He was very upset walking home with his head between his shoulders.

Andrew felt sorry seeing Peter in this way, but he could not do anything about it.

He looked left and right, back and in front of him making sure nobody was following him. No one was. Walking slowly due to heavy bags, Andrew took a rocky path where it led to a green hill. It was a remote area where it was pretty dangerous and beautiful. The hill was cursed that is why it was dangerous.

The village named the hill "The Death Trap", because if anyone went there he would die in a fatal accident except for Andrew. He had been walking in "The Death Trap" for the last two years and he had always come back without a scratch.

Andrew loved "The Death Trap". There was so much peace. It was so beautiful. Andrew could relax under the old oak hearing birds singing and smelling the fragrance of the flowers. He was even gladder there was nobody else who could reveal his dream.

All the books and strange metallic parts Andrew bought were in the old rotten shred on top of "The Death Trap". They were hidden very well so even if anyone would enter the shred he would not find them easily.

He spent all his spare time after school and at the weekend until the sun was setting. His family was not worried about all the hours Andrew was spending outside. Probably they thought he was playing with his classmates or best friend. They did not know that Andrew had fallen out with Peter.

For the sake of appearances Peter behaved as if nothing had really happened between them. Peter covered up a lot of the times when Andrew could not explain where he had been saying to his family "Andrew has spent all afternoon with me playing in my garden" even though that was a lie.

Andrew was actually inside the shed of "The Death Trap".

Later on that day in his room, Andrew was whispered to Peter: "Thanks for today. Please do not ask me where I have been" and Peter would not do that and find out anything.

Three years passed, Andrew had been moved to a different class with talented classmates. He did not feel displaced. He had learned a lot from the books he bought. He knew usually more than the old teachers. He had been feeling very uncomfortable in the old classroom. The kids used to laugh at him for his knowledge and intelligent. He felt like a fish out of water. "It is bad to be the best in the class"

Being relocated to a new class was wonderful, because he could talk to the kids, who had the same intelligence and knowledge. Andrew did not feel alien now. Even the new teacher respected him very much. The old teachers were so horrible to Andrew. "They are jealous of me" "I know more than them"

Andrew was learning more complicated maths, mechanics, physics and astronomy.

Other school hours were dedicated to physical and mental sports. Andrew loved all more than before. His favourite hour was the chess club. He had never played it before. He thought it was a boring game. The new teacher explained "chess is a fantastic game of strategy, brain and learning power" "You will not enjoy it at first, but the more you play, Andrew, the more your intelligence will grow with your capacity for learning and self-improvement"

"Yes sir"

The years went by. Life was becoming more difficult for Andrew. Apart from his part time job and time spent in the shed of "The Death Trap", his family wanted and demanded more time to be spent as a family.

Andrew had no choice but to tell lies to his family for keeping his dream alive. Andrew did not consider them as lies but as out of proportion excuses.

He remembered the time when he told to his family about Thomas, an invisible friend, who had lost his mother. Thomas needed a mate to talk to and Andrew was there by his side. Andrew had to spend all afternoon cheering him up. Thomas wept all the time. He could not understand why his mum was dead.

"She was so young. Why has God taken my mum away?"

"Aw. I know Thomas I am sure your mum is watching over you. You have to be strong so she can be proud of you!"

His family believed him completely. They were easily deceived or maybe because Andrew was very good at it. It was the way he told the excuses playing with the emotions and plausible reality.

Even though Andrew had a vivid imagination, it was becoming very hard to come up with new excuses. He even recycled some of them with gaps of time otherwise his family would start to be suspicious.

Andrew so lucky that his family could "drink" excuses like water and they had a poor memory.

This was playing in his favour. Anyway his dream was getting closer and closer to be fulfilled.

He was very careful not to be caught at night. When everyone was asleep, he got up in the middle of the night and went to the shed.

His family and big brother did not wake up as they were sleeping very deeply. Most nights Andrew could not sleep anyway. They were snoring too loud all night. He had tried to make them stop, but nothing had worked.

Andrew was not upset with them. On the contrary he was very thankful. He was able to make great progress to his dream. At the same time he avoided questions and found excuses.

Despite working at night, his school and work hours were not effected by the sleepless hours.

His adrenaline was keeping him very active. He never overslept or was late for school.

Andrew knew his life was changing for the better. It was a question of sooner rather later.

Andrew could not believe the years flying by so quickly. He did not care at all. He was excited. Eight years ago when he started his dream he thought he would never succeed on finishing his creation. Now he only had to make few adjustments and it would be ready for testing. He did not know if it would work.

"One thing is theory the other is the practice"

It was coming up to his sixteen birthday. Everybody was so excited but Andrew he wasn't. He didn't bother. "Who cares, I won't be here" "They don't care about my birthday. They behave like that pretending I am very important"

"It's the same every year" "They remembered me on my birthday" "What about the other 364 days in the year?" "Where were they?"

His family was preparing a huge buffet for Andrew's friends and relatives. They paid a magician, a DJ for the party. "Who will turn up to my party?" "They don't know I don't have any fiends"

"They will be very surprised when no one turns up!"

Andrew had other worries on his mind. He needed to find other excuses so he could escape from this imprisonment. His family was tormenting him with many questions about the party.

Andrew was not coping very well. If he did not go out soon, he would blow up like a volcano doing something silly and regretting it for the rest of his life.

"Sorry mum, I have to go out or I will explode"

"Andrew what about the balloons… what about the cake?"

"Mum what about them… you decide I am happy with anything"

"Andrew don't say that, come on, help me it's your birthday"

"It's still 6 weeks away. We've got time"

"I don't like rushing things. I am a perfectionist. I like organising everything so everything will go smoothly at your birthday"

"Thanks mum. I have to go now. We will talk later"

"Always later Andrew. That's why you are undecided"

Andrew slammed the front door without saying one word back.

"I hate my mum when she behaves like that" "She is such a perfectionist. I cannot live this life any longer" "Soon I will be out of here" "Life is full of surprises. You cannot make plans" "Something will come up and your plans will be out of the window"

The only place Andrew was happy was the shed. Seeing his creation made him smile. His face was lit up with joy.

"In six weeks I will test my creation. I hope there are no hiccups and everything will work."

"It should be ok!" "Fingers crossed"

Six weeks were not long to wait. It is like saying "piece of cake".

His birthday coincided also with the prom at the school. It was a very chaotic day. Meanwhile Andrew was at school, his family was making the last arrangements for his party.

Andrew was not himself. His thoughts were miles away. He was arranging his day completely opposite from his family.

The last thought was his birthday. He was preoccupied with his creation. There were some risks involved that he had never considered before. He was not scared. It was normal to have doubts on the crucial day, which could change Andrew's life forever. He had to be stronger and faithful everything would be fine.

"I have worked so hard to achieve my creation and it would be silly to walk away now"

With this reinvigorated faith in himself, Andrew heard a shout.

"Andrew, are you here with us?"

He was the maths teacher. He had behaving very badly since his wife left him for a millionaire. He used to be a very understanding person who loved his students and helped the community. Since then the maths teacher kept loosing his temper without any reason.

"I think he is still angry that his wife left him in this way" "She was always so faithful and a loving wife until her mother died."

"Nobody knows why. Some of the nosy neighbours heard she was complaining that her husband was too poor"

"Sorry sir" "I could not understand this exercise"

"That is odd, Andrew" "You have been the best of my class for years and you can't understand this simple exercise?" "Are in love, Andrew?"

"No Sir" "My family has been stressed me out about my birthday for last six weeks"

"I see"

"John, please explain this exercise to Andrew"

"Yes Sir" "Andrew it is simple. A-B in bracket multiply CV/43R"

Andrew was not listening. His thoughts were in the shed of "The Death Trap" with his creation.

After that hiccup, Andrew had a better day. He did not have anyone tormenting him all day long.

After school, his family welcomed him with balloons and wishing him "Happy Birthday" as soon he entered the front door.

Andrew was quite surprised some of his friends were there. They were dancing and giving presents to Andrew. He smiled at them, but his smile was false. He could not understand why they had turned up. "The previous years they never came to my birthdays" "Maybe they turn up for the food or the magician and DJ" "I don't blame them. We have a massive garden where you can invite your relatives and friends for your wedding banquet"

Andrew did not remember anything about his birthday. He did not listen at the magician or the DJ's music. It seemed they were talking very slowly and from another world.

The day came to an end. Andrew received a kiss from a girl he had never met and 10 presents. He had a slice of his favourite lemon cake covered with whipped cream. It did not taste great. It didn't go bad. It lost his flavour. It seemed to be in a black and white movie where you don't have sense of smell, taste and hearing.

Andrew was getting ready for the school prom. He was in the bathroom for his final touches. Little bit of gel in his black and curly hair made him very cool. He never bothered about his appearance. He just pretended to his family he was going out and he would have great fun.

Andrew was wearing a black jacket, trousers and shoes. Underneath his jacket, he was wearing a posh shirt with long sleeves and black bow.

"Andrew, it's late. Come on. Hurry up. It is half past seven", his mother was shouting from downstairs.

"Your friends are here, waiting for you!"

"I'll be there in a sec", Andrew replied.

"What is the rush?" "Nobody will notice me tonight" "As soon I go to the prom and everyone sees me. I will go to the shed"

Andrew walked down the stairs slowly. One step after another sounded like a long goodbye. At the bottom of the stairs Andrew looked back for a long minute trying to remember all the best memories he had in the house and his room.

"Andrew, here you are" "You look so good I'm sure you will break a lot of hearts tonight"

"Mum, you are embarrassing me" "Stop it"

All of his family was in the living room. His big brother was smiling at him. He was proud of him. His name was Stephen. He was 10 year older than Andrew and was getting married next month. May was getting warmer every single day. Stephen had met his fiancée in the same school that Andrew was attending. Stephen had never left her. They were soul mates. Her name was Jennifer. She was very beautiful, long curly blonde hair with an amazing smile. "If you felt sad, her smile would make you smile too." She had a very curly figure. "I am not surprised my brother is getting married. I would do the same if I were in his place"

Stephen was hoping his brother would be lucky too. They had never argued in 10 years. They always got on very well. Andrew had a secret plan for his future. He never revealed it to a soul.

His mum and dad were proud of him for other reasons. They could see him growing as a future adult despite they had reservation as a person. They still believed Andrew was not ready for relationship commitment and responsibilities for lack of maturity.

Andrew was mature and wanted to prove it. He was waiting for the right moment. He looked at his mum and dad for the last time and winked at them. "Despite of the bad time we had I still loved you. Please remember me" "Please don't cry for me. I'll be ok" "I'll always look down where I'll be!"

Andrew was thinking loudly.

"Go Andrew!" "Your friends are still out!" his dad shouted.

"I'm going"

Andrew rushed out of the door. His friends were waiting outside very crossed. They had been waiting for at least half an hour.

"Sorry guys! My mum is a pest. She did not let me leave. She told me a lot of final recommendations for the prom"

"Ok Andrew. Get in! We still have to pick up the girls" Peter answered back.

In the car, Joseph was sitting on the back. "Who is this guy?" "I don't know him" "Maybe a friend of Peter?"

"I'm sorry Andrew. Joseph this is Andrew, my best and oldest friend, Andrew this is Joseph, my brother"

"Nice to meet you Joseph"

"Nice to meet you Andrew"

They shook hands firmly.

"Which girls we have to pick up tonight?"

"Steph and Lorraine", Peter replied.

"Nice girls. Rumours were spreading I fancied both of them. Of course that was a lie. I did not have any feelings for anyone. My passion was my creation"

They were cheerleaders of the American football team "Lyons". They were very beautiful girls with blonde hair and green eyes with slim figures. Everyone fancied them, but they were not keen on boys. They enjoyed their own company. Some were saying they were lesbians. That was a rumour it had never been proved right.

They were wearing white dresses with matching shoes and bags. Their hair was in a ponytail to the disappointment of the guys except for Andrew.

"Guys, if you are asking about the lesbian rumour, we are not joining you. We'll ask Steph's dad to take us to the prom"

"Don't worry girls. We won't. We are gents"

"Ok guys?"

"Yes Peter"

"Ok Peter"

"Thanks guys. It has been a very stressful week for us. Everyone was talking in the school and no one gave us any peace"

During the journey, no one talked. The guys were afraid to talk in case they brought up the subject or said something silly. Steph and Lorraine were too shy and not talkative girls.

Andrew enjoyed the silence.

They arrived at the car park and a crowd surrounded the car at the sight of Steph and Lorraine.

The crowd followed Steph, Lorraine, Andrew, Peter and Joseph inside the prom. They wanted to find out if the rumours were true. Peter and Joseph were enjoying this short fame. Steph and Lorraine went straight away dancing. The music was very groovy. The DJ was playing in the latest pop songs.

Andrew smiled. His chance came unexpectedly. Nobody would notice his earlier departure from the prom as all the attention was concentrated on Steph, Lorraine, Peter and Joseph.

Andrew walked out of the back door.

He was so excited. The time had come to test his creation. He jumped along the rocky path leading to the shed of "The Death Trap". "I cannot believe tonight I will test my creation"

"Not one of my family, best friends or police will find me!" "Tonight my life will change forever" "I will not come back" "I will be gone forever"

There were not doubts in Andrew's mind. He knew what he was doing. He opened the door of the shed. He entered inside his creation. With his fingers crossed, just a sign of good luck, Andrew turned the light and the engine on. The engine made a very low pitch. Hi creation was a very metallic composition in a saucer shape. Andrew was overjoyed. So far how his creation was responding. "So far my creation is working well" "Let's see what happens when I move the controls"

Andrew moved the controls of the spaceship. The spaceship went forward and upward in a fraction of second breaking the speed of sound. Andrew had a quick look down, the last goodbye to his planet Earth. He was not sad nor did he regret his choice. He was delighted. He was in space. "Other planets and galaxies to explore. I can't wait" "Let's see how fast my creation can go", moving the control further.

The spaceship went into hyperspace and it disappeared into the billion lights of the Universe.

Peter and Joseph had a fantastic time in the prom.

They danced and got drunk. They were so drunk, Mr Brown, their teacher, had to take them home.

"Peter what a night. We have been so lucky. Anne kissed me and gave me her number"

"Yes Peter what a night" "I was kissed by someone I didn't even know" "Do you know where Andrew is?"

"Is he not with you, Joseph?"

"No. He is not with me. He was definitely with us in the prom. I don't know what happened to him" "Mr Brown, have you seen Andrew?"

"I've been looking for Andrew in the building but he is not here. He probably went home earlier"

Next morning horrible news spread in the village. Andrew was missing and the police were involved in finding him. They were looking for him everywhere even over 50 mile radius. Andrew's family was devastated and confused. They could not believe their son had disappeared. They were looking in the wrong way. They should have looked up. Andrew was somewhere else. Only he would know where he was, but for the first time he was enjoying every minute of his life. Nobody would be tormenting him and he would learn more of the Universe. Andrew would never come back and learn what future had in reservation for his family. He wanted just to fulfil his dream: flying in the Universe. He had done so. He was so proud of himself. During his exploration, he recorded into his computer all his knowledge experience as a testimonial of his life's achievement.

LUCAS AND DORIS

Lucas was woken up by the sunlight of the new day. Unaware of the future events ahead he was feeling very happy. Doris' perfume, an intense lily fragrance, scented the bedroom.

Her dressing gown was lying on the bed. Lucas picked it up and smelt her. He closed his eyes. She was there.

The passionate and intense love that had happened the night before had changed Lucas' life forever. He had been single for a long time, but now he had found his soul mate.

He looked around. Doris was not in the bedroom. "Doris, where are you?" Lucas shouted.

His voice echoed in the million pounds yacht, but there was no response. Lucas looked at the clock. It was midday.

He became increasingly worried and concerned.

Doris should be home by now, but she wasn't. "Where was she?" "Did something happen to her?" "She never stayed out so long"

Many questions and thoughts overcrowded his mind.

A terrible feeling came over Lucas. Doris was in danger and he was the only person who could save her.

With no time to spare, he got dressed and started to look for her.

He knew Doris was going shopping.

"She told me last night before I fell asleep"

Despite searching in every grocery shop and supermarket, none of the staff remembered seeing Doris that morning.

It is a small town in a small island. I am sure someone must have seen Doris.

She was 5'6" tall with blue eyes and blonde hair. She had a slim figure and was wearing a pink dress and shoes. No one seemed to have seen a woman with this description.

"Maybe she forgot about going shopping and she went to visit Carlos"

This thought gave a boost to Lucas' spirit and morale. He convinced himself that was what she had done.

"We all met up and laughed about her imaginary disappearance"

Carlos was a friend of long standing.

He had a villa with swimming pool overlooking the sea.

Although Carlos hated living there, he loved being at the seaside for health reason.

Carlos suffered from asthma and the sea air made him feel better. "It is the fresh and clean environment you need", the doctor recommended.

"Hi, Carlos How are you?"

"Hi Lucas I'm fine. Thank you, how are you?"

"I'm worried and upset"

"Why, Lucas?"

"I am looking for Doris, but I cannot find her anywhere. I went to the supermarkets and grocery shops, but no one had seen her, have you?"

"No. Last time I saw her was last night. Maybe you could try to her favourite café. She might have met an old friend and had a drink"

"Thank you Carlos. You have been a great help"

"You are welcome Lucas"

Again Lucas set about searching for Doris, but he was getting more upset and frustrated. In all the cafés and bars the same answer emerged. No one had seen a woman of that description.

It was possible she had passed unnoticed or it could be that something terrible had happened to her. It seemed for Lucas that the second possibility was the more realistic.

Then an idea came into his head. "Of course", Lucas shouted, slapping his forehead which was cold with sweat.

Some of passers-by stared at him thinking he lost the plot.

"She might have felt ill and been taken to the hospital"

From the pocket of his jacket, he took out his mobile phone.

"Come on Doris… come on Doris be there…"

Lucas was thinking pressing the button of his mobile phone nervously.

His worries seemed to fade momentarily and a new hope rose again.

Again the bad news prevailed. No woman of her description had been taken to the hospital.

"At least she is not ill or badly injured, but where is she?"

"I do not know where to look. I have been searching everywhere and I cannot find her. She has simply vanished from the face of the earth!"

After being walking around for three hours, with tired legs, low morale and worried face he found himself outside the police station. Another hope was shattered, with dismay he walked inside.

The police station was crawling with activity. The telephones were ringing continuously, but no one answered them.

The cops were too busy to restrain two disruptive tattooed criminals who had been arrested for bank robbery.

The two convicts were swearing and reluctant to be incarcerated so four policemen had no choice but to drag them by force into the cell.

While this was happening, a constable was sipping his coffee watching the scene and the smell of the fresh coffee brought Lucas back to reality.

"Good afternoon, Constable Smith"

"Good afternoon, Sir"

"My name is Lucas Dominguez. I have been searching for my girlfriend Doris Rodriguez all afternoon, but I cannot find her anywhere"

"When did you last see your girlfriend?"

"Last night before I fell asleep"

"At the moment sir, it is too early to involve the police in this matter. We have a policy of 24 hours for people going missing. No unless you know someone wants to harm her"

"Not as I know"

"Do not worry sir. I am sure she will come home soon. Probably she is home now and is wondering where you are"

"Thank you, Constable Smith"

"My duty sir"

Lucas walked home with renewed hope. He arrived and dreamt that Doris was running towards him hugging and kissing him all over.

Constable Smith was wrong.

He walked into the kitchen and found a shopping list on the table.

To buy: eggs, potato scones, unsmoked bacon and milk.

"Where is Doris?" The same question was going round and round his head.

She was wondering the same. She woke up in a dark room filthy and horrible smelling.

A half-eaten rat was lying down dead near her. The smell was horrendous and nauseous. Other rats were ready to attack their friendly corpse, but they were afraid. They were staying at a safe distance.

Doris was not scared at all.

She was feeling great and disorientated at the same time.

"How did I get here?" "Where am I?"

On the corner of the room the light of a new dawn was coming through a gap of the wall.

Doris was desperate to escape the mysterious and terrifying adversary. She knew her life was in danger.

She looked around to find a get away.

Meanwhile the light was slowly approaching her, a door nearby was opened. In a flash she flew through.

The other room had the same horrendous and nauseous smell, but there was no gap in any wall. Doris felt safe.

She looked herself in case she was hurt.

She noticed there was a stain in her pink dress. She touched it and she was shocked.

"That's blood!" "How did it get there?"

"Where is Lucas?" "Last time I saw him was last night"

"I can't recall what happened after that"

"The only thing I know is I can't go out. I don't know why I'm afraid"

"My instinct tells me my life is in danger. I will die if I do"

"I will wait until sunset"

Doris did not feel hungry or thirsty. She knelt on the floor all day long.

On the other side of the island, more frustrated and worried Lucas had a brilliant idea, sitting and smoking his pipe in his rocking chair on the wooden deck.

He felt peaceful and had a serene smile in his face. The rocking chair reminded him of his childhood. In his early years he had cried many times and his mum knew that rocking the cradle was the only way to make him smile.

After all the previous failures, it seemed this time he would succeed in finding her.

Lucas had a friend whose name was Jose Santiago. Jose was a private investigator and in many years had cracked very difficult cases, which the police had not managed to solve.

His instinct and intelligence helped him on many occasions seeing the entire of a crime where instead the police had fragments of it.

In a powerful positive state of mind, Lucas dialled Jose's number.

"Good morning Jose. It's Lucas speaking"

"Good morning Lucas. How cam I help you?"

"I had been searching everywhere for my girlfriend, Doris Rodriguez, all day and talked to anyone I know. I've even spoken to the police, but they could not help me. There is a 24 hour policy for missing people"

"That's right, Lucas. Hmmm. That's weird. Can you tell me more about her?"

"Doris is a 5'6" blue eyes and blonde hair. She has a slim figure and is wearing a pink dress and shoes. She is also 29 years old with a beauty spot on her neck"

"Thanks Lucas. Just a moment… I'm checking on my laptop. With this description, only one woman is coming up. Her name is Doris Rodriguez, but …" The three minute suspense was killing Lucas.

It seemed an eternity. "…She died 40 years ago"

"That's absurd. Doris is 29 years old. Something is not adding up. Are you sure Jose your laptop did not make a mistake?"

"My laptop had never failed in 20 years."

"I don't understand, Jose"

"I know Lucas. She might have lied to you about her full name"

"She might, but I'm pretty sure she told me the truth"

"In any case, if you wish I'll use all my resources to find her"

"Thanks Jose"

"It's my duty. My fee is £10,000. Lucas"

"That's fine"

"I'll call you with any news, Lucas. Goodbye"

"Goodbye Jose"

Lucas was very confused. Jose was right. He had never been wrong in 20 years.

"Could Doris have lied to him? Or could Jose's laptop have not been updated with the latest information?"

Lucas was certain Jose would eventually find her.

Despite his many doubts, Lucas was calm and relaxed sitting on his rocking chair waiting for Jose's phone call.

The day flew at an incredible speed. Sunset was approaching. The shadows were becoming longer and a cold breeze was blowing.

Doris did not move all day. She was still kneeling on the same spot. She felt happy. She knew the sun was disappearing below the horizon.

Darkness was winning the battle against the light approaching in every direction.

The cold breeze turned sinister causing all the people of the island to shiver. It was so creepy to be outside no one dared walk in the streets.

They had been taught by word of mouth for 100 years: "Never go out in a sinister breeze otherwise you will die"

The legend was narrating "creepy evil creatures would escape from their graves, walk and kill innocent people at night!"

No one could confirm it if it was a true or imagine story as nobody had dared walk in the streets and if someone had done so no one had come back alive to tell!!

The streets were ghostly as so chill, it made the skin crawl.

Creepy evil voices echoing in every part of the small town. "Kill, kill everyone", they were whispering.

Doris was not frightened at all.

She noticed not a single soul was out and about. The houses were dark and silent making the atmosphere more unpleasant.

In the middle of the air a burning cigarette was hiding in a black alley.

Doris continued her quest through the sinister breeze.

Meanwhile Carlos was admiring at the sea. He did not believe in the legend. He thought the legend was an imaginary story for frightening the children.

He was unaware of the danger.

Doris saw him and in a flash she appeared surrounded by black clouds behind him.

Doris whispered "Hi Carlos" kissing him on the neck.

She stared at the new moon shining.

"Kill him, kill him", the voice whispered louder in her ear.

A power evil force invaded and possessed her.

Her teeth and nails turned longer and sharper.

Doris was ready to bite, but… a whistling sound flew through the air and something struck her back.

"Oh, dear" Those were her last words.

Her body turned to ashes.

Carlos turned his head around.

"Doris, where are you?"

Nobody replied.

The following day, Lucas was sitting on his rocking chair sipping a Bacardi and coke still waiting for Jose's phone call.

An anonymous envelope arrived.

Lucas opened it and found a gold necklace with an inscription "Love you always Doris", a wooden sharp stake with some ashes and a piece of paper "Doris will never come back. Please pay £10,000"

Lucas cried for few minutes. His tears rolled down his face. With his right hand he dried it.

He realized Doris had gone forever and he had to live without her.

So he decided to leave these painful memories and sad island and cross the sea for the rest of his life. Nobody has ever seen Lucas again after he disappeared beyond the horizon.

Expect the unexpected

Martin O'Brien was an ordinary man. His life was so ordinary that every day went the same way.

Martin went to work on the bus and walked for 20 minutes in the office in the city centre of Glasgow.

His job involved phoning to people arranging appointments for windows, doors, conservatories and door garages to be replaced.

The job was not great. Martin was getting continuously abused by people, who insulted him or slamming the phone down on him. His job was not a selling job, it was a market research. The people were getting the phone calls, they did not understand. Probably they were tired of getting phone calls when they were too busy or expected an important call or they were about to go out for work.

Martin was trying to explain to one person "This is no a sell phone call. It is just a market research"

"Do not care, go to hell"

Martin looked depressed putting the receiver down.

He needed the money so badly. His bank account was always over drawn. The money was coming very handy for paying his rent, travel and food.

The company was paying him £4.50 an hour, which was illegal as the minimum wages were £5.52 an hour, but Martin did not have the courage suing the company demanding them on increasing his wages as he was scared he would loose his job.

Times were tough. There were no many jobs. Martin had been looking for a job for the last three months. He had used all his savings for paying the rent, food and utility bills. The money ran out miserably. Two weeks ago Martin took the last paper on Monday morning which advertised jobs.

"If I do not get a job soon, I don't know how I am going to pay the bills" Martin though.

He had no much choice. He made few phone calls; unfortunately all the jobs had been taken except for one.

It was the market research. "I don't have anything to loose"

"Good morning, my name is Martin O'Brien. I would like to apply for the market research vacancy advertised in the paper"

"Good Morning Martin O'Brien. That's great. We have interviewed slot tomorrow morning at 11:00 am. We are at Bothwell Street n°3 in the city centre of Glasgow. The dress code is smart"

"Thanks"

Martin was jumping with joy. "I can't fail. They take anyone even people do not have experience at all"

The next morning Martin arrived a half an hour earlier at the interview. Despite of being nervous, he got the job.

Martin came home and he was feeling more enthusiastic of his life. "At least I do not have to be worried any more about money. I will have money to pay my rent, food and travel and have some for me"

Martin lived alone in his flat. His family died many years ago. He never had a girlfriend. Martin was a very average guy. He was not ugly or handsome. He never had girls chasing him when he was younger.

"I never cared about girls. I heard from my ex friends all the troubles they had been trough. Some of my friends married the wrong woman, who married their husband for money or committed adultery after 4 weeks of marriage"

Martin did not have that trouble. He did not sleep with a woman for a quite while. He was a not virgin. He lost his virginity when he was 16 years old.

His mum and dad did not know when and where it happened.

Some weird letters were coming to the post. Martin did not recognise the sender. They were all good news.

One sender apologised Martin saying he forgot to pay him last week and he would pay him by cheque next week.

Martin was puzzled. He scratched his head and he did not understand.

"I do not know who this guy is. I am sure it might be a mistake. He confused me with somebody else"

The next week a letter with a cheque for £300 arrived payable to Martin O'Brien and he cashed it into his bank account. "Maybe it may be my lucky week" Martin thought.

"I do not care if this guy made a mistake I cashed the cheque and if the right person demands this money I will say I never got it"

Things turned weirder every day.

One day when he went to work an old big and short woman approached Martin. She looked 51 years old and she was like an apple shaped.

"Martin, do you remember me? Is Michelle?"

"Sorry, have you confused me with somebody else?"

"No, it is you Martin O'Brien. You made loved to me last week in my apartment. I just came to see you for warning you; my husband knows everything about us! He is furious like a cat! He wants to kill you! Be careful"

"I truly do not know that woman. I definably never made love to her. I do not care about her husband"

"Something weird is going on. Things are happening to me and I do not know why"

"I am not a man with a lot of sex appeal and women chase me. I am not Richard Geare"

Martin shrugged his shoulders and head.

He went to work and he had a normal day of abusing and poor results at work.

"Next day will be better than today" Martin thought and hoped.

On the bus a stunning lassie with long legs approached him and whispered in his ears: "Since his last time I saw you I cannot live without you. I dreamt of you"

"I do not know her, but I do not mind"

Martin did not care and he was pleased. Something was happening to him. "Finally after an ordinary life, things are changing for the better"

The lassie was called Jennifer. She was 6' tall with long legs, a curvy figure, green eyes and short hair.

Martin let Jennifer into his apartment and without a minute to loose, they both took the clothes off and made love.

"She must taking drugs and sleeping around and she confuse people"

Something came into Martin's head. "Could it be possible somebody else looks like me and he uses my name and do all the things I have no done pretending to be me?"

"There could be a twin brother somewhere with my same face I did not know. My dad and mum never told me"

"Certainly I have to expect the unexpected"

Martin's life turned fantastic. He got married and had two children. He never got divorced and he found also a well paid job. Martin was very happy and thankful for everything came into his life.

THE TRAVELLER

Joseph Loser was not a lucky person in word and in real life. In his entire family he was the only one. His sister Sarah had won the lottery and scooped £1,500,000.00.

His oldest brother Mark was running an International company in Brazil and his wages were £100,000.00 a year.

His mum Samantha was helping her husband Martin in their restaurant in Monaco and the restaurant was very lucrative business around £1,200,000.00 a year. They were both bringing home £250,000.00.

Joseph was unemployed and without a penny in his bank account. He was really a loser. He could not do anything right. He could not even get a girlfriend or keep a job for long than a week.

"I feel so hopeless and inept"

To make things even more depressing, all his friends were better than him. They had great jobs, money into the bank and stunning girlfriends or wives.

Joseph did not have anything at all.

"I wish I had a bit of luck in my life. Just a bit, I do not want too much. I would like to have some money, a girlfriend so my family and friends will get off of my back and stop laughing at me"

"It is so depressing and humiliating having these people treating me in this way"

"I have done everything I can. I have applied for jobs, but I can't last longer than a week and I can't get a girlfriend. I am a nice guy. I treat women like they are princesses." "Nowadays women like being treated badly and they think nice guys are boring" Joseph thought.

"There is nothing wrong with me"

"I am tall 6 feet. I have got blue eyes and brown hair. I am lack only of confidence. Apart from this, I am good a honest and handsome man"

Joseph mobile phone was vibrating on the bed.

It was Patrick. Patrick was his very old friend from school. Patrick was very clever. He did not care about money or women. He was only interested on his inventions. He was obsessed. He was spending all his time, energy and money.

"Hi Patrick are you doing?"

"Hi Joseph I am great thanks" "I am so happy"

"Why is that Patrick?"

"I finally succeed to complete my invention"

"Really Patrick, what is this time?"

"I can't tell you over the phone. Maybe someone is listening. We need to meet"

"Okay, tell me when"

Patrick was worried someone could steal his inventions and made money, but the worst part was taking all his credits. That is why Patrick secretly invited Joseph in his lab and only Joseph knew where it was.

Patrick trusted Joseph with all his heart and he knew Joseph would never betray him.

Joseph wrote down the time, took his jacket and went out.

He knocked the door twice.

"Are you alone Joseph?"

"Yes I am"

"Did anyone follow you?"

"No, trust me. You are the only friend I have. I would never do anything to jeopardise our friendship you know that"

"I know I just want to make sure. These days never trust anyone"

"I know Patrick"

Patrick opened the door and Joseph closed behind him.

"What is this time?"

"This is an amazing invention which could change history forever"

"Wow I am intrigued"

Patrick went to his a secret room and came back with an object wrapped into a small blue silk blanket.

Patrick unravelled the objected.

"Double wow" Joseph shouted and putting his hand in front of his mouth in a way to say sorry for having shouted and someone could have heard and came to see what it was.

The object was a screwdriver with a blue beam.

"This is not an ordinary screwdriver. This is a travel time screwdriver. If you turn this knob up, you will go into the future and if you turn down, you will go into the past"

"I understand Patrick"

"Have you already travelled?"

"Yes I have Joseph. The things I have seen. They are amazing"

"Just a moment Patrick, what if you change the past and future you will create a paradox"

"I know that and don't worry nothing has changed. Do you think I am that stupid?"

"I am sorry Patrick"

"No problem Joseph, I phone you because I want to help you"

"What are you going to do, Patrick?"

"Everyone knows you are unlucky"

"Yes sure rubbing in it Patrick"

"…and we are going to change that! I am going to send you into the past with a mission of betting many sport events knowing already the results so you cannot loose"

"Right Patrick good plan I like that" Joseph's eyes started brightening up.

"I have here in almanac from 1970 to 2000" "What you have to do just bet some money into the winner in any sport you like, but be careful do not bet more than two in a betting shop otherwise they get suspicious"

"Ok thanks Patrick"

"I am bit worried. Are you sure it will work?"

"Do be a chicken now Joseph"

Patrick selected a date 12/04/1970 in the screwdriver and gave it to Joseph.

"Simply press this button and you will travel to this date. When you want to come back just turn up the knob and select a date okay Joseph"

Joseph closed his eyes pressing the button and a sucking force took him into the past. Joseph disappeared into a thin air.

"Good luck Joseph" Patrick said.

Joseph found himself in the past and with a stake of £10 he made £3,000,000.00 in a week.

For Patrick 50 seconds had passed by when Joseph came back with the news.

Joseph appeared from a thin air.

"Hi Patrick, looked how much money I have"

"I know Joseph. You should have been more careful. You have brought so much attention to yourself"

"I am sorry Patrick"

"Next time I will be more careful"

"Yes next time. I want to explore time and space"

"No you won't."

Patrick ran towards Joseph in order of stealing the screwdriver from Joseph. Joseph knew what Patrick intentions were. "I won't give up the only thing has changed my life forever". Joseph turned down the knob and selected a date and disappeared into a thin air.

Patrick never saw again Joseph. He read all his adventures in books and magazines. His name was all over the World.

Certainly Joseph Loser was not longer meaning that anymore he was recognised as a man could not fail as failure was not acceptable.

CHRISTOPHER AND SIMACO

Christopher Matthews was born on Friday 13 April 1917.

His family knew his son would not be different from them. He was born unlucky like the rest of the family. It had started with the great-great great-grandfather in 1780 when he lost all his fortune in a gamble business since then all the males in the following generations had tried to turn the misfortune around with very risky gambles.

All their attempts failed miserably. "This curse will never break up" "It will carry on forever and ever throughout the generations", Sebastian commented loudly to the family. He had failed too in his life. He had a great idea for making money. His idea was very well thought through with constructed financial bases limiting his costs at the minimum so he could make a high profit. Sebastian knew though the curse would find a way to strike his business. He hoped this time would be different. He would break the curse.

Sebastian had a friend called Frank. Frank was selling import gems from South Africa to Sebastian. They were very cheap as no one knew these new precious stones, but as soon as the demand increased there was more competition causing the price to fall, thereby reducing Sebastian's market.

Sebastian foolishly reduced his prices too. That was the last straw for his great business. With high losses he had no choice but to borrow money. He borrowed like there was no tomorrow. His debts eventually caught up with him. They spirally higher and higher until he had to sell his house. Now he lived with his wife, Clara, a twelve years old daughter, Sarah and his new baby boy Christopher under the Healthy Bridge in a carton box. They did not feel cold or miserable. They were very adaptable in these new circumstances. It was very weird The Healthy Bridge brought a lot of money for Sebastian when he was selling the South African gems and now it was his poor home.

Sebastian did not forget what his grandfather and father told him before they died. "Son, whatever you do the curse cannot be broken. We have tried and failed" "The more you try to be rich, the more you will become poor"

"The best way will be, just leave it. Enjoy what you have and do not ask for more"

It was not that simple. It was an obsession for the Matthews. If he broke the curse, good luck would run through the future generations on and on. His chance was lost. He knew he had no way to get his fortune back.

"When the curse strikes you, no matter what you do it will not let you get back your feet again"

"My only hope is my son, Christopher"

"He was born on a bad day and year" "We have no chance" "Sebastian was thinking"

Despite the poor conditions, the Matthews would not give up. They made the best with what they had. No one of the community helped them with clothes, food or a place to live. They were completely alienated. They couldn't understand why. Christopher did not miss either toys or sweets. He had gorgeous vivid blue eyes. Clara had never seen such gorgeous eyes in her entire life.

The oddest thing in Christopher was not his eyes, but his hair. It was ginger. In the entire Matthews's history, no male or female child had ever had ginger hair. It was very peculiar.

"Do you find the colour of Christopher's hair very strange, darling?"

"Yes, my dear. I have never seen anyone in my life with ginger hair, certainly no one in our family.

Christopher's hair is unique and rare" "Could it be a good sign?"

Certainly, it was not a good sign for Christopher since everyone teased him about it.

"Look at the ginger boy!" or "Come on ginger!"

They were upsetting Christopher and he was getting angrier and angrier. There were occasions when Christopher lost control and pushed people down the street or turned upside down the café tables. Some of the passers-by had no choice but to call the police to the scene. Christopher would run off before they arrived. He was a not a bad boy. He was just tired that his life was so difficult. He wanted to be someone very important so people would respect him. He was really fed up.

"Christopher, stop moaning"

"Mum, I'm fed up living here. Can't we have a house, food, clothes like everyone else?"

"Son! Be grateful! We've got each other and that counts more than anything else" "Our love is bigger than material possessions"

"I know dad" "but… you don't have people laughing at you for your ginger hair"

"People envoy you, because you are different"

"No, I'm not different! I'm beggar"

Sebastian's face turned red with anger. "Christopher, go and come back with an apology for your cheekiness!"

Christopher was feeling sorry for his cheeky words. He did not mean it. He did not want to see his family in this situation. He wanted to help, but he did not know how. His dad told him about the curse. "It is all in vain" "How can I help my dad if I am unlucky like the rest of my family?"

As he was walking down the street Christopher saw something shining between the stones. It was a silver coin. Christopher picked it up. It was a shilling. "It's a brand new shilling" It was so shiny. He had a strange vibration and metallic reflection holding in his hand. "My dad will be proud of me for this small fortune"

"No, do not spend me" "Please keep me"

Christopher looked around. There was nobody else except him and the coin. "Is there anyone behind that tree?" No one replied. Again the voice spoke. "I'm here in your hand. I am a lucky coin"

"You make a wish and I will grant it"

Christopher was very confused. "Was it possible a silver magic coin could exist?" "Could it be a fruit of my imagination?" His stomach was rumbling. Christopher hadn't eaten a proper meal for long time. "That's right! I am starving and I hear things!"

"I know what you are thinking" "I am a magic coin and I can speak"

"If you are real how?"

"I used to be a genii in a bottle and an evil witch transformed me into a silver coin" "I defeated her, but for revenge she put a spell on me!"

"I see" "What is your name silver coin?"

"Simaco"

"Nice to meet you Simaco" "My name is Christopher Matthews"

"Nice to meet you Christopher"

"You are a mess. Christopher"

"I know Simaco" "My family is very poor and we live under the Healthy Bridge"

"Christopher, have you always been poor?"

"No Simaco. My dad used to have a house, food and clothes, but we lost everything because we are unlucky" "We have been under a curse since 1780" "The curse can be broken by a male of the family and our misfortune can be turned around" "The thing is... I don't know how"

"I know how Christopher" "Destiny brought me here today"

"That's right!" "I will take you to my dad"

Christopher was running around the people in the street. His feet were burning hot and he was feeling wobbly. "I am feeling sick, but I need to speak to my dad" "Simaco is the only way to break the curse" Christopher knew that running out of breath.

"Sorry... dad" in a husky voice. "I am so sorry"

Christopher was catching his breath.

"I accept your apologies"

"Dad, I have great news" "I had found a shining shilling in the street"

"That's great son"

"This is a magic shilling"

"Magic shillings don't exist" "I don't want to hear it" "This is the last time you tell me stories"

"Ok dad, I will" Christopher replied lowering his head with a sad face.

"Darling, you have been too harsh to Christopher!"

"My dear, I haven't. I don't want people to think Christopher is demented"

Christopher did not blame his dad. He had told so many imaginary stories that his father could not take them anymore.

"It is a shame my dad didn't let me explain" "He would understand" "Why didn't you speak up Simaco? You could have helped me out!"

"Sorry Christopher, the only person who can hear me is you!"

"The adults don't believe in geniîs or witches!"

"So what now!"

"Christopher, have you forgotten?"

"I can grant wishes" "Just rub me and make a wish"

"How many wishes?"

"Three"

"I need to think. I have only three wishes. I cannot waste them"

"Don't worry Christopher. Take your time. Don't rush straight away"

"Thanks Simaco"

"You're welcome Christopher"

Christopher was in a very sticky situation. He did not where to turn. "Should I choose to be selfish by making myself rich or try to help others?" After much thought, Christopher decided.

"Simaco, I've decided"

"Please tell me more Christopher"

"I want to be rich. I want to be important so people will respect me."

"Are you sure, Christopher?"

"Yes, I am Simaco" "I can always do good"

"Yes, you can" "So what is your first wish? Christopher"

"I wish... to be the richest boy in the entire world"

Christopher closed his eyes as tight he could. It was a strange feeling. It seemed like waiting for a present you know is coming to be wrapped up. Christopher was so excited. He could not wait any longer.

"All done, Christopher"

He opened his eyes slowly. He looked around, but nothing changed. He was on the same spot wearing the old torn clothes with bare feet with muddy face, arms and legs. Christopher looked at Simaco with angry eyes and face. "Simaco, you have disappointed me!" "You said you can grant my wishes" "I'm still the same poor boy"

"You're a fake"

"I'm not a fake. Be patient Christopher"

"Why should I keep you?"

"Christopher, wait until the morning…"

"Ok, I will. If you fail me tomorrow, I will throw you into the river. Is it a deal?"

"Done deal Christopher"

Sebastian came back with some bread, beans and fruit. He lit the fire and cooked the beans inside a rotten pan. His face and hands were muddy. He had lost a lot of weight like all his family since they had become poor. He had a hacking cough. It was getting worse every single day.

"I think my dad will die pretty soon if nothing happens out of the ordinary"

Sebastian had begged all types of weather: fog, heavy rain, burning sun, and freezing cold and blistering snow.

He was desperate. He would do anything to keep his family fed. Sebastian could only just survive on the money they had.

With years going by, life was becoming very tough for everyone and the offers became less and less just to eat beans, some fruit and bread.

Water was in abundance as they were living near a river. The river was drinkable. They used it to wash themselves. They enjoyed it when it was a hot summer day. They just jumped inside keeping themselves cool. The problem was they had to share it with everyone else. They did not mind. The Matthews were very understanding and easy-going people.

"I hope tomorrow Simaco doesn't let me down. If I am the richest boy in the world, we won't have to live like this anymore"

"Christopher, where have you put the shilling you have found?"

"Sorry dad, I think I lost it" keeping the coin in his right fist behind his back.

Christopher didn't like telling lies to his dad. He had no other choice. Simaco was becoming a very valuable friend.

"I cannot give Simaco away" "Apparently Simaco said it can grant wishes" "If it doesn't, I can always give it to my dad tomorrow morning"

"Christopher, never mind"

Christopher was still starving after dinner. He could not get any more food. The night brought a very bad storm. Christopher was so tired he didn't hear the thunder and the heavy rain falling. He fell asleep and was only woken up by the sun of the new day. Something felt really weird. He could smell flowers. "Where is this fragrance coming from?"

"There were not growing flowers near the bridge" "It was all cement base" "There was grass, but it was at least a couples of miles away"

Christopher's eyes were not completely opened. The image was pretty blurred. He was half-asleep and half-awake.

He scratched his head. He couldn't understand where he was. Then he rubbed his eyes in disbelieve.

The lilies were inside a glass vase on a bedroom cabinet.

Christopher had slept on a comfortable goose mattress and pillow. The bed as made of wood and the bed linen was French made of wool with a swan and lake drawing in the middle. Christopher pinched his face.

There was a man at the far end of the room and he was drawing the curtains with the same identical pattern.

The room was so enormous in size Christopher could image himself dancing. The ceiling had an angel pattern.

"Wow, what a beautiful room!" Christopher threw his bed linen and he was amazed. He was absolutely clean. He had never seen his skin so pink before. He was wearing new cotton pyjamas.

"Good morning, Sir" the man said after finishing drawing the curtains.

"Good morning"

"Would you like to have breakfast in bed, Sir?"

"Yes, sure" Christopher was feeling so comfortable even though he didn't know where he was.

He went out of the bed and followed the man whose name was Jimmy and who was to be his personal servant, apparently.

His bedroom was situated on the south side of the house, as it was warmer and bigger than any other room.

Christopher stopped for a moment to look at all the paintings, statues and suits of armour in the long corridor. He had never seen so many beautiful objects in his life. His dad had mentioned them to him. He was always listened carefully imagining what it would be like if he could be rich.

Christopher touched them making sure they were real. "I'm not dreaming" "They are solid and cold"

On the side of the corridor wall Christopher admired a decorated glass. "I don't have time to waste." "The man is walking down the stairs" The staircase was made of mahogany with a handrail and angel half boost balusters, white marble covered by a red carpet. Christopher was so excited. He ran down the stairs missing some of them as he jumped two at a time.

At the bottom of the stairs, Christopher found a floor of mosaics, the large wooden front door, a long corridor leading to the kitchen, study, dining room and the garden.

"It would take me ages to explore all house" "I hope I am not sleeping" "Please don't be a dream, be real!"

"Good morning Christopher" "Yes, it's all real"

"How Simaco?"

"That is my power to grant wishes"

"So I'm not dreaming" "It won't disappear it will be here forever" "No unless…"

"Please not unless what Simaco?"

"If you wish it not to be here, it will vanish, Christopher"

"No, I won't Simaco" "Can I lose it though?"

"What do you mean Christopher?"

"I mean like my dad when he lost everything"

"Anyone can lose everything. You are in control of your life. It's up to you what you do"

Christopher was delighted. His dad would be proud of him.

"My dad will be so happy. I have succeeded in defeating the curse and becoming rich"

Christopher remembered something. "The curse cannot be defeated" "It will come back and take everything I own"

"Unless…" "I wish for it"

"Simaco I have decided to make another wish"

"Are you sure Christopher?" "I am reminding you there are two wishes remaining"

"I know Simaco. I wish I have luck"

"All done" "Your wish had been granted"

"Great! Let's go and see what happens!"

Christopher cannot wait for the result. "If I succeed, I will have broken the curse"

"Hello Sir"

"Hello"

"My name is Jimmy, your personal servant"

"Hello Jimmy"

"I see you have decided to go down for your breakfast, sir"

"Yes Jimmy" "But before I have my breakfast I would like to ask you if you could place a bet for me"

"A bet Sir?" "It is too risky" "You have money. You don't need to bet"

"Jimmy, please help me"

"Certainly Sir" "I'll bring the newspaper"

"Thanks Jimmy"

Jimmy brought the newspaper Daily Star dated 3rd April 1925. Christopher turned the pages very fast. He was looking for the sports section. He stopped at the horse racing. "That's the one!" "It's the horse I want the bet on at £1000 to win" "Bowl Coaster to win"

Christopher was so agitated. He knew he was going to win.

Jimmy looked at the name of the horse. "Are you sure, sir?" "Bowl Coaster is 300/1 to win" Can I advise Best Mate?" The bookmakers give him as 3/1 to win"

"No trust me Jimmy" "Bet Bowl Coaster"

"I'd better hurry. The racing is on in 20 minutes"

"What about the £1,000, Jimmy?"

"Sure Sir" "I will show where the safe is"

Jimmy and Christopher went to the safe behind the painting in the study. Jimmy took £1,000 and closed the safe.

The study was full of books on shelves. Next to the leather chairs facing the marble fireplace, a transparent globe contained bottles of spirits.

Jimmy didn't lose any time. He went straight away out.

Christopher noticed a radio in the study. He had never seen it one like it before. Christopher was very curious.

With impatience, he started pressing all the buttons. "I want to know if I'm lucky"

The radio was on. "At last"

"Today… We are at York races for the Gold Cup 3 miles at 14:45"

"We have Best Mate at 3/1, Rusty Buster at 7/1, Beau at 8/1, Seal at 10/1, Never Lost at 2/1 and last Bowl Coaster at 300/1" "What do you think about the race, John?"

"No doubts, grass is firm, Never Lost is on top form and it had strong legs. I bet my house on it!"

"It's the bookmakers favourite no chance for Bowl Coaster"

"It's simply out of place amongst these stallions"

"They are ready on the stall and they are off"

"Never Lost is first, second is Seal and third is Best Mate and the pack follow. Last is Bowl Coaster"

"With 2 miles to go, Never Lost is still first followed by second place Seal and third place Best Mate" "Bowl Coaster is still trailing last"

"Come on Bowl Coaster" "Go go go Bowl Coaster"

"What a minute" "That's incredible! Bowl Coaster is flying" "Bowl Coaster is overtaking Rusty Buster on 5th place"

"With 1 mile to go, Never Lost is still first followed by second places by Seal and Best Mate, but the horse of today is Bowl Coaster now overtaking Beau on 4th place"

"What a race! Are you excited John?"

"Yes Andy" "This Bowl Coaster is coasting to win" "An outsider is really going to upset bookmakers"

"With half mile to go, Never Lost is head at head with three horses: Seal, Best Mate and the horse of today Bowl Coaster"

"Go go go Bowl Coaster" "Go Bowl Coaster to win"

"Last two fences to go, incredible Never Lost is slowing down" "Probably Never Lost is too tired. It has been leading the entire race"

"Bowl Coaster is leading the group. Second place is between Seal and Best Mate. Bowl Coaster has one fence advantage from the second and third place"

"The spectators are delirious" "I don't blame them who would guess Bowl Coaster to win"

"Bowl Coaster… Bowl Coaster is the winner followed by photo finish Seal and Best Mate and last Never Lost"

"What do you think, John?"

"It was a thriller, Andy" "Congratulations to Bowl Coaster"

"Yes John, congratulations to the horse and jockey"

"Apparently, there is only one winner who betted on Bowl Coaster. His name is… Christopher Matthews who wins an incredible £300,000"

"Congratulations Christopher Matthews" "I don't know if he is lucky or he knew Bowl Coaster was a winner"

"Yes I won" "I broke the curse" "We will be lucky forever and ever"

All the noise woke up his dad who ran down the stairs.

"Where are we?"

"It's our house dad"

"I don't believe you, son"

"It's impossible" "Let's go out before the owner kicks us out"

"Dad, trust me we are the owners and I broke the curse"

"That's impossible" "No one of the our family has broken it"

Jimmy returned home with £300,000 and gave them to Christopher. Jimmy confirmed Matthews were the owners of the massive villa with ten bedrooms, three bathrooms, a kitchen, study, attic and 100 acres of garden surrounded by trees and flowers and a swimming pool.

"Hip hip hooray" Sebastian was overjoyed. Sebastian was dancing and jumping in the air. He could not wait for telling his wife and daughter the great news. He ran up the stairs.

Christopher heard screams of joy. They were dancing too.

Christopher knew his life had turned around and he would never be unlucky again. There was something else Christopher had to do before his life was completely happy.

"Simaco, if you had a wish, what would you like to wish for?"

"Christopher, I would like to be free again breathing the air, walking on the ground and have friends like a human being!"

"I wish Simaco becomes a real boy"

"Thanks Christopher!" The coin was all wet. Simaco was weeping for happiness. A bright light came out of the coin turning into ashes. The corridor was underneath a white fog.

"Simaco, where are you?"

"I'm here"

"I'm afraid, Simaco"

"Don't be" "Soon the fog will vanish"

As soon Simaco said it the fog vanished into thin air and a twelve-year boy appeared in the corridor.

"Hello Christopher, what do you think about my new look?"

"You look great Simaco" "How about changing your name?"

"I agree" "How about Perry?"

"Hello Perry"

Perry was a twelve-year old boy with blonde hair and blue eyes.

His eyes were so blue they seemed to say, "I am free" "I want to breathe and walk around"

Perry didn't wait longer. He had been imprisoned in the coin for the last 400 years. The world had changed a lot since he was a genii. He wanted to know and live.

"Thank you Christopher. You have given me back my life" "How can you reward you?"

"You have done so you made me rich and lucky"

"You made me free Christopher"

Perry ran out of the front door. Christopher never saw Perry again. He imagined Perry was still travelling around the world, learning, meeting new people and eating local foods.

Christopher took his life very easy. He got married in his twenties with Anita and he had two children, a boy Andy and a girl Jennifer. He lived for 104 years happy and lucky.

His luck was transferred from generation into generation.

"That's right my grandson", Anita said.

"You are lucky as your granddad and your wife and children will be too"

"I would like to know granny how you met granddad?"

"My dear that is another story" "I will tell you tomorrow"

"Give your old granny a cuddle"

Little Daniel approached her granny and gave her a warm cuddle.

"Thank you Daniel"

They both fell asleep and dreamt about Christopher "The luckiest and happiest man in the world"

LUKE ANDERSON

Luke Anderson had all. He had a lucrative job working in his lawyer firm in Hollywood. He had sex appeal with short blonde hair, deep blue eyes and a smile could make women to fall to his feet. He came from a rich family. His father like his grandfather was a lawyer from generation to generation and they were so successful they never lost a case. They were very clever men they knew when their clients were lying. They analysed them and if they felt their clients were liars, they would not take the case.

All his life Luke had always been chased by women. They loved him as they found him so down to earth and kind. He was not interested in women as yet as he was fully concentrated in his education. "There is plenty of time to settle down" "First I need to become a qualified lawyer then I find a woman"

As his father and his grandfather, Luke attended the New York University of Law where he exceeded with the highest result. During the time Luke spent in the University, he met Clara, in her late twenty, who wanted to become psychiatry. She loved helping people to solve their personal and emotionally problems during traumatic experiences. Clara was gorgeous with curly blonde long hair and very slim figure. All the male students were so in love with her. Clara was on the other hand was not interested. She was so absorbed in her study, she would not engage with anyone.

She loved law and astronomy. On the day Luke and Clara met, she was walking and so distracted with family problem, she crashed against Luke. All her books fell in the foot path and Clara fell backwards.

"Are you ok?" Luke asked with a warm smile.

"Yes, I am sorry it's my fault" Clara blushed.

"Do not worry about it" "Give me your hand I help you to stand up"

"Thanks"

Clara's heart was beating very fast. She felt so confused and embarrassed.

Luke felt the same. He did not what to do or say. He never had a girlfriend before like him as well Clara had not had a boyfriend either. The chemistry was really strong and profound. They spent so much time together studying law and found out they both loved astronomy.

After the graduation their relationship bloomed so deeper they got married in New York and they moved to Hollywood.

Clara's family was rich as well and her father was an accountant. Clara was preoccupied about his father Armstrong Carter during the time of recession as he could lose everything he had. Her father managed to overcome his financial problems and Clara returned to be more serene.

Clara and Luke bought a mansion house with an electronic gate and mermaid fountain in front of the house.

Luke was still being a lawyer even though he did not need to. He had one million dollars in his bank account, but he loved too much his job and wanted to help other hopeless people, who nobody wanted to represent them legally. He stopped charging people. He did for free. Luke had enough money he bought several cars for each occasion and state of mind and mood. He had a convertible Ferrari 512BB, black Mercedes Benz, a silver Lacetti Chevrolet and even a limousine for special occasions and VIP entrance.

Clara loved her Ford Fiesta. It was so easy to drive and park.

God blessed their love. It was so pure and ever lasting. They had two clever daughters. The oldest was called Jennifer, five years old. She wanted to become a pianist and the youngest called Jessica, three years old, wanted to be like her father a successful lawyer.

In the hottest day of summer Luke has driving his Ferrari. He was feeling the breeze in his hair. It was three o'clock and Luke had finished to see all his clients and just wanted to spend time with his family in the pool.

All the neighbours were so jealous of Luke. They wanted what he had. His house had one internal swimming pool for winter and an external one on the back of the house, a pool table room, four bedrooms, a large family kitchen, two bathrooms and two reception rooms.

Luke did not care about the house that much, because the most important for him was the people living in the house.

Luke pulled over the car in front of the house.

He opened the front door and shouted "Honey I am home"

Clara came first to welcome him home wearing a bikini "Hello darling, how was your day?"

"Wow you look as beautiful as the day we met"

"Thanks" Clara blushed.

"It was all right, busy as usual. Come and give me some love"

She rushed without a minute of hesitation. She hugged and kissed him.

As soon as Jessica and Jennifer heard her dad voice, they ran from the back of the house, where they were swimming, into the hall and hugged their dad legs.

"We love you, dad"

"I love you too. All of you are my precious princesses" "I will be the happiest and rich man in the world if I was poor, but I still have all of you in my life"

Luke felt incredibly happy and satisfied.

Ding ding the alarm clock went off.

It was eight o'clock in the morning.

"No, no again" "At the best moment, the bloody clock went off" ""It was so getting interesting"

That was the dream and Luke had to go back to reality. In real life, Luke was not married. He never had a girlfriend. He was not even a lawyer. He was a qualified accountant, but despite his qualification he could not get the job he wanted. He had never been really lucky. He applied for many jobs, but he only got jobs nobody applied for. Luke did not care as he needed to money to pay the rent and food. He was not living in Hollywood either. He lived in Worcester in England and his house was not mansion house as you probably guessed. Trevor, the previous tenant, wanted to make some upgrade to the house without the knowledge of Stewart, the landlord. Trevor had made many holes in the walls. Some of the neighbours were saying he had a quick temper and Stewart did not sue him he was too scare of being killed so let Trevor scot-free.

Stewart could not repair the damages as the recession was damaging his business so hard he would just manage to keep it afloat.

Luke was all right with it. He was a very tolerant person and he did not mind about the state of the house.

He had a supposedly "pet" called Frankie. It was a mouse, but it did not belong to Luke. It just helped itself at home from one of the hole of the house.

It was the only real friend Luke had. He had long conversation with Frankie, but it was not very talkative. It was just showing itself if it needed food.

"It is late Frankie" "I have to go to work"

Luke got a quick wash, dressed and had two jam toasts.

Luke was considering lucky in a way. Many people had lost their jobs. Luke was still working. His job was very physical and tiring mentally. Every day after work he was complaining of continuous and acute headache.

He was the only one who was suffering from it and still working. Many of his colleagues were in such pain they called in sickness. Some others had been diagnosed with brain tumours derived by the noise of the workplace.

Luke was working in a building site and his duty was making holes with pneumatic drill. Even though Luke was wearing a safety helmet and headphones, they could not prevent from brain tumour for long exposure of the pneumatic drill.

It seemed the vibration, high sound and long exposure of the pneumatic drill was causing damaged to the user.

Luke was not afraid about the danger. He had not family and no relatives. His mother died giving him birth at the age of 30 and his dad died ten years later when Luke was only twenty.

Luke knew that is the destiny of each human being. "We are born, we live and we die" "That is our destiny"

He was very positive person and took his life how it came.

Luke had some other friends in the building site. He liked John and Rob. They had beautiful wives and daughters.

Luke could not spend time with them after work. He was so tired. Some times after work he just wanted to sleep. As soon as he arrived home and saw the bed, he fell into the mattress and did not wake up until the next morning.

Luke knew something was wrong with him. He was too scared he would lose his job or not get paid by the employer if he found out he was too ill to work.

He kept working no matter what even when the pain was so unbearable.

Today was one of these days, the pain was so acute. Luke felt his head was about to explode. He stopped the pneumatic drill and put his hand on his forehead rubbing it pretending he was feeling hot.

One minute Luke was standing tall and proud in his thirties next minute he felt like a sack of potatoes on the gravel. Luke woke up for thirty seconds and heard the voice of Rob calling him. His voice echoed in his ears. Luke felt unconscious again in a state of coma.

The building site doctor ran towards Luke trying to reviving him, but in vain. After all the failed attempts, John without a minute of hesitation called the ambulance.

Ten minutes later the ambulance arrived and the paramedics checked his pulse and eyes.

"Luke, can you hear me?"

Luke did not reply.

"We have to take him to hospital. He is not responding"

"Can we come?"

"Does he have any family?"

"No, he only got us"

"Ok then let's go"

The paramedics transported the unconscious Luke in the ambulance followed by John and Rob. The ambulance took ten minutes to reach the hospital.

John and Rob were so preoccupied about Luke's condition.

Luke woke up again hearing at the voices of the doctors and nurses around him.

"Where am I?"

"You are in safe hands" the doctor replied.

At the reassuring words, Luke fell asleep again with a serene smile.

Two hours had passed since Luke had fallen unconscious. He was lying in the hospital bed when he woke up. Luke did not remember what it did happen and how he did get there. He was so resting peacefully his battery was so charged up. He could take the world he did not feel any pain. Even his acute headache had gone.

"Hello Luke, my name is Keith. I am your doctor for today"

"Hello Keith"

"How are you feeling?"

"I'm feeling great"

"Good, I am pleased to hear that" "Do you know what happened?"

"No, I was working as usual and then I felt my legs went and all my body was switched off. After that I can't recall a thing"

"Yes, you were in a bad shape"

"Now I am feeling great"

"The reason you are feeling great I gave you a strong dose of sedative for your pain"

"I see"

"Do usually you have headaches, Luke?"

"Yes daily it is part of the job, everyone does"

"I work in a building site and all my colleagues got it"

"I have run some tests on you while you were unconscious … and … I am sorry to tell you I have got some bad news"

Luke knew what it was coming. He grabbed the bed lined with his right hand hoping not to hear the B T words.

"Luke, you have a brain tumour"

Luke looked down and with a strange smile replied "It is ok doctor. I will be fine"

The doctor was a bit surprise from his reaction, with warm and sincere words replied "I am sorry we cannot do much for you. If we knew your condition six months ago, we had a fighting chance to defeat the tumour, but at this stage it is so advance there is very slim chance you will survive. I feel so powerless"

"Do not worry Keith, I know you have done everything you can to help me"

"We can offer you some sedatives for the pain" "I subscribe them for you and again I am sorry I cannot be more assistant to you"

"Thanks Keith"

Keith was feeling so down and sad he could not do more for Luke. He just wanted to save everyone. "Some times you win some battles, but some others times you lose and that is life"

Luke had to stay in hospital for a week to recover and get used to self inject sedatives.

His job was gone as his employer had already replaced him with a new pneumatic driller unaware of the dangers of the new job.

Luke was thrilled he had three months to live and he was looking forward every day to spend in bed dreaming.

In few occasions John and Rob came to see Luke how he was doing. They were playing poker and having a beer meanwhile Luke was sleeping.

"Luke, how are you doing?" Stewart shouted from downstairs.

Luke didn't reply.

"Shall we see if Luke is ok?"

"Ok"

John and Rob went upstairs and entered Luke's bedroom. The room was unpleasant smelly like if the window had not been opened for a while. Luke was not moving lying face on one side covered by the bed linen.

"I hope you don't mind if I open the window Luke"

John opened the window. "It's nice air" "Can you smell the flowers?"

Again Luke did not reply.

"Should I check the pulse, John?"

"Why do you think he is gone?"

Cautiously and slowly afraid Luke could move Rob approached the resting body. He was still.

His body was cold and there was not pulse.

"He is dead"

Both Rob and John cried. They were sad no one had said goodbye to Luke before passed away.

Luke was happy instead, no alarm clock would interrupt his life again no headaches would torment him anymore. He would not wake up from his dream living with his gorgeous wife Clara and his two daughters Jennifer and Jessica.

He was the happiest man in the world living with his precious princesses and he felt his life was completed now.

OTHER PUBLICATIONS

The author **Paolo Debernardi** is going to publish these forth coming books and in the following pages there is description of what to expect:

"Idyllic paths Sentieri Idillici" Italian poetry and proverbs book with English translation

"Angelic Dreams" his first English poetry book

"Xandra the Destroyer" his first English Novel

"The adventures of PD" his second English Novel

"Idillic Paths Sentieri Idillici"

"Idyllic paths" is not just a collection of poetry and maxims in Italian with reviews and English translation, but is also a journey in which my emotions and daily life emerge and seek to communicate my suffering, hopes and quest for happiness in a language accessible to everyone.

In writing my compositions I have managed to find one of my dimensions and partially to satisfy that quest for happiness.

Through my words, I collect everything around me reproducing it in the same way.

In my biographical compositions themes and styles vary from youth to maturity.

Poetry dedicated to nature, the seasons and places follow poetry dedicated to Italian television presenters, the love for Miriana Trevisan and the friendship of Rosario Fiorello and Stefano Gallarini and to my sad life where suffering, paternal violence and the lack of affection from my family emerge in a dominant way.

Continuing to write, I realised that metre was suppressing my inspiration and originality.

Without obstacles, new poems sprang up with many varied themes: the sea, dawn, nature, the UFO and love are examples of this. Through my poetry I am sending a message to my contemporaries and future generations to enjoy and protect what surrounds us and to help our neighbours.

Thank you for the compliment you are paying me through the selection of this volume.

I hope that you like and enjoy reading "Idyllic Paths" and that you will read my future publications.

Paolo Debernardi(The Author)

"ANGELIC DREAMS"

The most striking element of these poems is the imaginative way in which the language is used. They illustrate very clearly the advantages of creating poetry in a foreign language. For in this situation one is not fettered by some of the basic rules that so often inhibit those writing in their mother tongue.

In this book you will find a great sensitivity to the sound of the language, most especially in such poems as "Fireworks" and "I belong everywhere". Here the combination of sound and rhythm greatly enhance the imagery.

One has the impression of travelling through a poetic landscape in which one looks at everything with new eyes. The poems "England" and "Soap bubbles" are examples of this "fresh" vision.

However by far the most moving aspect of this work is that it portrays a young person on the very threshold of life. For these verses exude all the joy, the pain and the vulnerability of youth. They show with considerable eloquence that special moment in life when one is aware of so many possibilities, which seem to be almost within one's grasp.

The hopes and the pain of almost, but not quite, realising one's dreams are all to be found in this collection of poems.

Young readers will have no difficulty in identifying with the feelings and imagery they will find here: - whilst those who are no longer in their first youth will recapture the emotions of that unique time in their lives.

David Sanderson (English teacher)

"Xandra the Destroyer"

"Xandra the Destroyer" is the first English autobiography novel, in which the author lives a difficult period caused by his ex and by his misfortune.

This is not only a book; it is also a way for the reader of understanding completely the author religiously, mentally and physically.

With this book, the author want to send a message to all his readers of being careful of not trusting in people, who we love, because sometimes they hurt us more.

The reader will find also there are friends, who had helped very much the author during this difficult moment of his life.

"THE ADVENTURES OF PD"

"The adventures of PD" is the second English novel, in which the author tells us the adventures of PD, a good God who had been chosen for saving the humanity from the badness and his evil brother DP.

If PD succeeds in defeating the badness and his brother, the goodness will prevail for the eternity, otherwise if he fails, the fraternity, friendship, equality and goodness disappear completely.

AUTOBIOGRAPHY

Paolo Debernardi was born on 3 July 1973 in Casale Monferrato (province of Alessandria) in Piedmont, but lived with his family in Mortara (province of Pavia, south west of Milan) in Lombardy until 1997.

In June of the same year he moved to Bishopthorpe and from there to York in England in the United Kingdom where he lived until March 2001.

For working reasons, he moved to Worcester where he lived until July 2002 and in August of the same year he decided to transfer to Glasgow in Scotland until 2006.

He moved back to York in 2006 and 2009.

From a small child he demonstrated his success, winning various awards in the Youth games in Mortara, in the painting and sports competitions.

A symbolic collection of medals, which took him to the Collegio San Carlo di Borgo San Martino as an accountant and commercial expert and discovered his greatest loves: football manager helping his teams winning several trophies and poetry, through studying the French symbolists Charles Baudelaire and Arthur Rimbaud.

Through these two great writers, a passion was aroused in **Paolo Debernardi** and this prompted him to write innumerable poetic biographies, maxims and dedications embracing different themes and styles to the point where they were put in a collection together with reviews from university lecturers, writers and the drawings of Salvatore Sepe in his first book, now out of print, entitled **"Saranno state le onde del mare d'inverno…"**[1] published by Edizioni Nuove Proposte U.A.O.C., (Union for Artists and Cultural workers) in Marigliano, Naples, Italy in November 1996.

Through his poetry **Paolo Debernardi** has appeared in many Italian anthologies having taken part in and won many prizes in a number of poetry competitions published in his native country.

He is also known in Germany and Australia at a local level and in the web page titled "www.storymania.com".

With his move to England and change in mentality, **Paolo Debernardi** has put aside Italian literature to pursue an immense challenge, albeit a more satisfying one, of writing poetry and short stories in English for the reason that English is a language spoken and recognised throughout the world.

Notwithstanding any difficulties, his determination and inspiration have enabled **Paolo Debernardi** to write English poems and short stories to such a degree of success that he came second in an English poetry competition published by The White Tower Writers Association in Doncaster, England and first in a poetry competition published in the town of Bova Marina, Italy.

His English poems has also appeared in several anthologies in Italy, Australia, Germany, England, Switzerland, Brazil and the web page entitled "www.storymania. com".

In 2000, **Paolo Debernardi** started to write English short stories and one entitled "They always come back" was published by the White Tower Writers Association in the review titled "The Partial Eclipse".

The three short stories entitled "They always come back", "Waiting" and "Delta Centauri" are also present in the web page "www.storymania.com".

---

1   [1] *"It will be the waves of the sea in winter…"*

On 07/11/2009 **Paolo Debernardi** auditioned to **Britain Got Talent** in Newcastle and he is still waiting for the result.

Besides writing this volume, in the future **Paolo Debernardi** will publish a volume of English poetry with review, drawings and colour photographs entitled **"Angelic Dreams"** and a volume of Italian poetry and proverb book with English translations entitled **"Idillic Paths Sentieri Idillici",** the first English novel **"Xandra The Destroyer"**, the second English novel **"The adventures of PD"** published by AuthorHouse.